*A Walk with
the Wind*

A Walk with the Wind

The saga of the First Nation
Shaman named Thunder

Norman O'Banyon

A WALK WITH THE WIND
The saga of the First Nation Shaman named Thunder

iUniverse books may be ordered through booksellers or by contacting:

iUniverse
1663 Liberty Drive
Bloomington, IN 47403
www.iuniverse.com
1-800-Authors (1-800-288-4677)

ISBN: 978-1-4917-9288-9 (sc)
ISBN: 978-1-4917-9289-6 (e)

Print information available on the last page.

iUniverse rev. date: 06/20/2016

Book 1

A Walk with the Wind

Table of Contents

Glossary of Medicinal and Edible Plants

Biting Bush: (Stinging Nettle) promotes healing, adds flavor, anti indigestion;

Bleeder: (Milk Thistle, stem or root) fights infection, regenerates digestion;

Bright: (Lemon Balm) reduces fever, relieves cough or cold, adds zest flavor

Cap Flower: (Echinacea) pain relief, fights staph infection, fever relief;

Corn for grinding into meal for cakes;

Dry Flower: (St. John's Wart) anti depressant, relieves headache, calms colon;

Happy: (Fern root) strong licorice flavor laxative, calms nausea;

Happy Leaf: (Mint) adds flavor, calms digestive track;

Juniper cones: crushed in boiling bag relieves chest congestion, coughing;

Little Seeds: (Oats) for grinding into meal for cakes;

Sacred Bark: (Cascara) calms nausea, laxative;

Seed Tree: (Filbert) edible nuts, leaves for smoking;

Smoke: (Leeks) adds flavor, settles digestion.

Discovery

Two furtive figures cautiously stepped out of the tree-line onto the pebble beach. Their eyes swept right and left, seeking any sign of other human beings. Covered in hide robes, they looked like part of the driftwood when they stood so still. Klaw and Helps were part of the Haida tribe, normally much further north, but they were on a scouting trip, seeking a new site for their village, one that would be more sheltered from the ocean storms. For three days they had gone in the direction of the morning sun. When they came, once again to the salt water, they turned right and had followed the shoreline for five more suns. Klaw, carrying a spear, bow, and shelter robes, searched for signs of food, while Helps, his woman, sought healing herbs and edibles. She too was carrying gathering bags and their meager food stores.

Even though the journey would have been more efficient had they walked on the open beach, they knew they could be seen, so they stayed in the shadows, with the woman frequently turning back into the dense trees and brush, looking for some new plant. Much of what she found was the same as the other forests had given, but every now and then there was a new surprise, which she welcomed, and shared with the man.

When the sun was at its highest, they stopped for a drink of water from their pouch, and chewed strips of dried seal. Klaw had been testing the wind; there was a sour aroma that was a sign of trouble. The woman nodded, pointing further along the driftwood.

By mid afternoon, the stink was much stronger. Klaw knew that they were nearing a place of trouble. He sat on a log to think about it. Helps, on the other hand, signaled him to come along; they were both needed. She was right, they were both urgently needed.

A half mile further, the stench was very strong, but they could not see the source of it. Finally, Klaw turned over an object that looked like a large stump. In fact it was a hide covered boat, the likes of which he had never seen. Underneath it was a frail form of a boy, covered in his own waste and vomit. His skin was cold and pale, his breath hard to detect. Klaw looked at Helps, replacing the shell as he had found it. "We have no time to waste on one who is so near death." He continued walking down the beach, but she did not.

"If this were your son, would you be in such a hurry to move on?" Her question was spoken softly, with respect for her man, but a plain intention to do something for this young one. "Do we have so many young men that we can fail to help this one?" She was turning over the leather boat once again; It looked to her like a very large basket with a vine maple frame. It was strange to her, but obviously well made. "Come on, Klaw, if you help me drag him to the water, I will improve his odor." She was smiling because she saw her man's shoulders shrug in resignation. He would grumble, but he would help.

They dragged the still body to the water's edge. Actually Helps knew she could have done it easily herself, there was so little weight on the hide the lad had used as a robe and cover. Helps began to flush the filth off the pale body; it didn't take long to learn that he had not been attacked or wounded. Meanwhile, Klaw went back to the boat to see what he could learn.

He found a walking stick that had a sharpened tip on one end and a heavier handle that could be used as a club in defense; a travelling bag had little in it, a few scraps of leather, some round pebbles, empty small food pouches, two small cutting stones and a small chopping tool. Klaw examined carefully the stone and the chipping of the sharp edges. It was unique to him, unlike the ones the Haida made. There was something like a paddle, but it had also been used to dig clams. And there was a pile of uneaten clams that were partially open and foul smelling. It also appeared to Klaw that some small crabs and a flounder had been speared and partially cooked and eaten. There was little doubt of the boy's sickness. He had poisoned himself with uncooked fish. Before he rejoined Helps, Klaw covered the site with seaweed and gravel to hide the smell as much as possible. If it had drawn them here, it could easily attract others.

Helps had removed the boy's deer hide breeches and shirt, adding them to the soaking robe in the shallow water. The frail body was rubbed first with grass and then rinsed. Even though there was a tiny protest, it was as if he might be swimming through a deep dream. She repeated the process, then rubbed him with a handful of fresh mint leaves, and rinsed again. The foulness wasn't gone, but it was much easier to handle. Helps did the same thing with the clothes. By the time she was satisfied, Klaw had found a suitable camp site up-wind from the odor, just inside the tree line. He had started a small fire with dry wood, which produced little smoke, and found some flat cooking stones.

The Trials

Fifteen days prior to that, Basket was trying to explain to her son the urgency of his preparation for the trials. Her persistence had out-lasted his father's who had simply said the trials would begin with the new moon, and further conversation would change nothing.

"Tswa," she said as patiently as possible, "the trials are for twelve year old men, to demonstrate your maturity. It is not a contest to determine who is the best; but rather a demonstration of how well you have grown."

Her son stood statue still, a deep frown on his face. "I am the smallest and least prepared to demonstrate anything. How can I wrestle with those who are much older and heavier than me?" He waved his hands in frustration. "How can I run as fast as those who have had almost an extra year to grow?" His voice was controlled by respect for her, but his feelings were very strong. "I haven't killed a deer or elk, only some small rabbits. How can I compete?"

"Tswa, it is not a competition, I told you. It is a way for Chief Bear and the Elders to determine the men who will go on the summer hunts." She was also feeling the frustration her son had. "But the trials only happen in the spring of your twelfth year. And Spear, your father is one of the Elders who must choose."

In fact, the trials were a rite of passage for young men. The challenges began with running and swimming, then hunting and fishing, exploring, and finally wrestling. It would take an entire moon to complete. Realizing the uselessness of further talk, Tswa turned toward the doorway saying, "I will walk with the wind for a while. Perhaps the wind can explain why I must be humiliated for the entertainment of the Chief and the Elders."

"Think more about it, Tswa," his mother said, as he paused at the door. "It is for no one's entertainment, but to find out who can best hunt and feed us, or protect our village from those who would take it from us." She watched his stiff back leave, a solemn silence in his wake.

As Tswa walked by the edge of the lake he pondered: "There is always enough food, more than we need." He threw a branch out into the water. "There is no other village on this lake, who would be our enemy? Who would try to take it from us?" But her logic was convincing; it was not a contest but a demonstration. He would simply demonstrate that he was not a hunter, or runner or fighter. "What then, am I?" he asked aloud. Another stick was thrown into the lake.

It had been a challenge to live in the house of Spear and his woman Basket. Three sons had been born to them and then two girls. Finally after two more baby boys were born and died in infancy, Tswa had come along. His name simply meant "four;" he was the fourth son of Spear. He often thought that he should have been named, "Kluil," "six." He was actually the sixth son of Spear. His two oldest brothers had women and a house of their own, but trying to stay out of the way of the two remaining men in the house was a challenge that Tswa thought should be in the trials. He was adept at dodging and defense. The thought caused a smile to brighten his mood. He walked and pondered through the sunset, and entered his house while there was still a hint of twilight.

Tswa tried to be quiet as he entered the darkening lodge, knowing that his sisters were already under their robes, and probably his mother and father, too. Instead he found the family gathered around the coals of the cooking fire. They were talking about the future of the village. It sounded as though a plan was at hand to move the entire village away from the lake to a stream that would provide available fresh water and a more sheltered area. Camas, his brother (who was formerly named "Three") was asking, "Can we move before the Potlatch?" It was the first Tswa had heard about either, a move or the Potlatch.

Spear tried to answer with an explanation. "That would depend on how quickly each family chooses their place. I think there are seven other Elders who would choose before us. Then, when we have a suitable place, it is only a matter of taking this shelter apart, and relocating it. With seven of us doing the work, it should be easy. But Potlatch is still only a suggestion." There were enough shadows that each person saw his expression differently. Since the dinner tray was empty, Basket rose to get Tswa a couple strips of dried deer meat, which was his favorite anyway.

His younger sister asked if the women would go to the Potlatch too. "Of course, if it happens," Spear answered, "There could be dancing, and a lot to trade, and many people to meet."

Basket quickly added, "But not to find a husband."

Both sisters giggled nervously, knowing that one day very soon, that would not be the case.

Tswa wanted to be included in the discussion, so he asked, "Father, why must we move so often? I can recall three other sites we have used."

Before Spear could answer, Camas said, "Because we fill the (waste trench)!" but he used the most vulgar term possible.

Spear chuckled, but Basket looked down, embarrassed for her son's crassness. Spear answered, "Yes, there is that, and," he sighed heavily, "and the fleas. They become such a problem it is easier to move than scratch all the time." All nodded in agreement.

Tswa had one more question, "May I go to the Potlatch as well?"

A long silence followed before Spear answered. "I do not want this to sound like a bargaining, or a demand. If you have a good trial, we will have a good Potlatch." The coals had nearly gone out, and the room was very quiet. "Have you given the trials more thought, Tswa?"

"I have, Father. I talked to the wind this afternoon. The wind told me an excellent plan. You can be sure we will have a good Potlatch." A sigh of relief fluttered around the room like a moth.

Three nights later, just as the full moon was rising from behind the big mountain, Tswa listened to the breathing of his family. When all were soundly asleep, he crept from his house as silent as a shadow. He carried his walking stick, and a gathering bag in which he had placed his sling, two small cutting tools and a small axe. He had some of Basket's corn cakes and ten strips of deer meat, a water pouch and a flint fire starter. He made his way to the lake where he had prepared a hide boat, usually used by the women, with a paddle and an elk robe in it. It was all he needed for his journey.

He pulled the round shell out into the lake, careful to step on the robe on the bottom fearing he might break a supporting bow, or tear the hide cover. After a couple pushes with his walking stick the depth was enough to sit down and paddle. A huge smile spread across his face. If the trial had included stealth, he would have passed with honor.

There was plenty of moonlight to see the tall trees, but Tswa was reluctant to head directly across the lake. He thought a safer route would be to follow the shoreline, which he did for about two hours. The moon was pretty high when he noticed the marsh, a dim gathering of grass and small plants that protruded into the lake. He continued to follow the shoreline.

The change was, at first, imperceptible. He noticed that his padding was more efficient; each stroke seemed to carry him farther. Then he noticed that the shoreline was getting closer, and he thought he had crossed the lake. When he stopped paddling he made his greatest discovery; he not only continued to move, he was actually moving faster. He had found the outlet of the lake and the headwater of a sizeable stream. In less time than it would take to shout for help, Tswa was ushered into the darkness of the forest on a body of water that had taken control of his tiny craft

Downstream

At first he was panicked, but then he realized this unforeseen discovery was helping in his quest. He was rapidly spreading the distance between himself and the trials that would begin in the new day. He could see so poorly in these deep woods that he seldom paddled at all; he just rode, and hoped for the safety of his little boat. Shadow forms of limbs overhead grew closer, and twice he was brushed by boughs. He decided that sitting upright was no longer necessary since he could not see which way to paddle anyway. He curled on the robe and sensed his little tub bobbing and turning on the currents.

Ahead, he could hear the tumbling water, but had little understanding what it might mean for him. Then, in a pulse-pounding rush, his boat tipped slightly and he slid down rapids, smooth rocks sliding under his hide boat. Then all was calm again with the fresh current. Two more rapid slides quickened his breath as Tswa was carried through the blackness. Once a large collision with a rock violently threw him against the hide side, but with a spin, his craft continued on toward some distant goal, undamaged.

It seemed to Tswa that the darkness was giving way to occasional glimpses of the moon and stars. The sky behind him was hinting at a welcome dawn. Then he heard the ominous sound of falling water, a sound he had never heard before, and would never forget. Moment by moment it grew in volume, then in an instant he had the feeling of being weightless as he was airborne. Fortunately, Tswa was leaning back as he went over the falls. The lead edge of his little tub did not plunge down, but stayed relatively flat in the descent. The splash folded Tswa in half, his breath knocked out of him for a moment, and a wave of water invaded his craft. As he gasped to regain his breathing, he tried to scoop the water out with his hands. Tswa sensed a calm that was new as he peered over the rim of the boat.

In the waning darkness, he could see reeds and bushes near the boat, and a low dirt bank in the distance. It seemed to him that the tall trees from his home lake had given way to lower trees and bushes, but his progress had not diminished. He was still moving, and gratefully not as dramatically. He resumed paddling in the direction the water wanted to go.

It occurred to Tswa that he had been in this hide boat for several hours. It was time to relieve himself, but he could not stand up to do it. Nor could he imagine urinating in his boat and then kneeling in it. He began looking for a place on the shore where he could land. Fortunately, a sandbar presented itself. Tswa smiled thinking, "The wind heard my need and sent me to this place."

In a very short time he discovered that it was more than a sandbar; it was the joining of another stream to his. When he carefully pulled his tiny shell onto the sand, he was surprised how stiff his legs were, and how urgently he needed to urinate. Once that was cared for, he studied the problem of marking his trail. It was never his plan not to return to his home. He needed some lasting help that would direct him to the proper stream.

A safe distance away from the water, so it wouldn't be washed away, yet still in full sight, he dug a deep hole with his paddle, and erected a large limb with a fork in it as a post in the sand. He then found a couple equally large straight limbs that he could rest in the fork pointing to the way he would find his home. When he stepped back to examine his work, he smiled. "Even the Elders would look favorably on his task," he thought to himself.

He turned the boat over to empty all the accumulated water from it; then enjoyed a corn cake before rejoining his journey. He had no idea how far he was going. The wind would tell him when he arrived. He realized it had been many hours since he had slept. Instead of making a camp on the shore, Tswa decided to simply curl up on the elk hide, and rest, as the boat drifted further along its way.

On and off, that same sequence of events happened for four days. When Tswa looked back upstream, he could see the familiar shape of his mountain across the lake from his home. Now, however, he could see that it was only a small son in a large family of mountains. He had eaten all the corn cakes and two of the deer strips. He had refilled his water pouch twice. The last time the water had a strong taste that he didn't like.

The morning of the seventh day, Tswa awoke to the smell of smoke. Alarmed, he hurriedly looked for the source. Ahead of him he saw another large sandbar, and across from it, in the trees a spiral of smoke suggested a village. He thought about passing the opportunity to mark his route, but realized it would be easy to confuse the fork in the river. He was as quiet and as quick as possible in leaving his marker. No barking warnings by dogs, or shouts of guards led him to the assurance that this was a wise choice. In the gathering daylight his little boat was around the bend before anyone from the village was awake or concerned. He had just entered what future explores would name Howe Sound.

Tswa knew that his progress was slowing. He did not understand that now in tidal water, he was no longer being carried on a river current. Now he was dealing with tidal movement. For six hours he could paddle with the outgoing tide and make good distance, but then for the next six, it was against him and he struggled to advance at all. During one of those struggling times he felt the wind puff from behind him. His light little boat seemed to surge with the boost. An idea was born.

When Tswa felt the wind behind him, he held the elk robe up for the wind to blow against. He moved faster than paddling! Tswa tested moving the elk hide at angles to the wind and was delighted to learn that he could modify the direction a bit. If his right hand was forward, the boat moved to the left; the left hand forward made it move to the right. And it was considerably easier than paddling. He watched the sun set behind the mountains ahead of him.

If he slept at all, it was in short naps, always waking with a start to search for some point of reference in the darkness. Inevitably the sun rose again over his mountains at home. Two more days passed while Tswa waited for the wind to tell him he was nearing his journey's end. Without warning, it began to rain, gently at first, but then with soaking vigor. Ahead of Tswa there was a prominent point, beyond which the water stretched vastly, the far shore nearly out of sight (The Strait of Georgia). He tried to direct his boat to that point and finally had to paddle furiously to settle on the pebble beach.

The boat was dragged up the beach by an exhausted Tswa; he had not had a full night's sleep in ten days. As soon as he could turn the boat over, and wedge it under an overhanging driftwood limb, he wrapped the elk robe around him and crawled under the craft, into a cramped, damp, but purely secure space. He slept soundly until the morning.

Perhaps it was the wind speaking, or the rain pelting down, Tswa knew he had to eat the final dried deer strip and continue his journey. He was able to fill his water pouch from the new water puddle on the top of the boat, and in a brief pause, he drank his fill from more rain. Before he left, he thought it would be good to make a large marker that he could see from a distance on his return. When he could think of no other reason to hesitate, Tswa dragged the boat down the beach, surprised at how much new slick green grass had grown, and how evident the brown weeds now covered the water. Once in the boat, he wrapped the elk robe around him and settled in the bottom of his tiny shell. The wind would decide his direction.

The rain muted the dawn, drained the color from the morning, hid the afternoon, and hurried the darkness of evening. Another day passed and Tswa was not sure how much progress had been made. He slept fitfully, listening for any tell-tale sound. His thoughts inevitably went back to his house, and Basket, who would be very worried about him. Spear would have searched for any sign of Tswa, perhaps even asked some of the trackers to help find him. He was also aware how precarious his situation had become. He was now lost in the middle of an enormous lake, out of food with no prospects of finding any soon. A grimace held his face. In an attempt to avoid the trials, he had placed himself in a much greater one, which had the additional condition of survival itself.

With the dawn the rain stopped and the breeze became fresh, but more from his left than from behind him. It was not pushing him toward the distant mountains where the sun went at night, but further into the huge lake. He lifted the elk robe for the breeze, and pushed his right hand forward. He had little to judge by, but it seemed to him that he was headed in a good direction. The shore seemed about a half a day's walk away. He was sure he could make it.

Tswa did not understand why the water seemed to flow into the lake some of the time, and then after a while, flow the opposite way. But he kept his attention on the shore that was drawing closer, if at an aggravatingly slow pace. Finally when the day was ending, Tswa used the paddle for the final distance. He slid his boat up the pebble beach to the driftwood, and once again turned it upside down, securing it with a limb. His stomach protested the thought of another skipped meal, but he was too weary to worry about it. He would find food in the morning.

He awoke slowly, snug in the elk robe. He listened for the wind, but there was none. He listened for the teasing voices of his sisters, the song of his mother, the grumble of the men talking, but there was none. Tswa crawled out from under his shell to find an overcast morning. The beach that he had crossed last night was now twice as wide with a wet sandy strip before the water's edge. A large flock of shore birds were scuttling about on the sand, apparently finding something to eat. Tswa reached for his collecting bag; perhaps he had found something edible too. He found the strap to his simple sling, inserted a round stone in its pouch, then whirling it twice, he sent a projectile at the flock. Most of the birds flew a short distance away, alarmed by the sound of impact. In a puff of feathers, however, one of the birds became a welcomed breakfast.

He hurried to gather his kill, then searched for a dry piece of cedar bark. With his axe blade he scraped away any sand and dirt to find dry wood, especially that with pitch on it. Then he scraped more vigorously to form a ball of fine fibers. With his flint he sent sparks into his work; soon a spiral of smoke told him his success was near. A few more gentle puffs and flame appeared. Quickly Tswa applied small dry twigs, then larger branches until he was convinced he had a good fire going. He skinned and dressed his breakfast, remembering to add more fuel to his welcome fire. Basket had always chosen a fresh stick to cook meat over the fire. Tswa searched into the brush until he found one just right. As he twisted his roasting bird over the flames, Tswa reflected that the trial judges would be impressed with his cooking abilities. He smiled, but also because his stomach was about to be satisfied.

Now that the question of food had been satisfied, he needed to explore for edible greens and fresh water. Armed with his walking stick and gathering bag, Tswa entered the tree-line, keeping the hint of a morning sun at his back. He found some fresh fern spurs, and some marsh reeds that had doughy centers. He was no longer hungry, now about water. He traveled slowly about two bow-shots further when he came to a vigorous stream with excellent water. After drinking his fill, and filling his pouch, Tswa reversed his direction, and after a while, was delighted to find himself on the beach, within sight of his boat.

There was a considerable amount of sand beach in front of his site. He placed more wood on his fire, and made a circle of rocks to protect the embers. Perhaps he could keep it burning all night; there was certainly no scarcity of available wood. It was then that he noticed the spurt of water from the sand, a big spurt. His curiosity on full alert, Tswa walked on the sand. He noticed many holes; then just in front of him, a large one spurted. He marked the spot and knelt to scrape the sand away. Nothing! He scraped more and found a hard shell. As he tried to release the shell from the sand, he could see that it was larger than he expected. With stubbornness, he wrestled the large object free. He had no idea what he held in his hand. It was hard and as heavy as a rock might be; but he was sure there was something alive, and edible, within it.

He carried his prize up near the fire, where a striking rock was slammed against the shell. The top half of it shattered easily, and the flesh inside drew back from the light. Tswa placed the rock on the fire. There was little movement, but eventually the juice began to bubble and Tswa was captured by the sweet aroma. Using the forked cooking stick, and another branch, he lifted the rock back out of the fire. His small stone cutter freed the flesh from the rock and with only a tiny hesitation, he ate. It was incredibly good! Tswa smiled broadly, "Just think in one morning I have fed on sweet reeds, a bird, and a stone! I wonder what the judges would think about that." He saved the bottom of the rock, which appeared to be a useful tool for later.

For four days Tswa lived in abundance. There was more food than he could eat. An excursion just off the beach in water so clear he could see fish on the sandy bottom, produced even more. The sharpened end of his walking stick speared a flat fish, and a creature that looked like a giant insect with pinchers, and tasted wonderful when toasted over his fire. He used his shovel to find smaller living rocks and placed them on the fire rocks. When they were cooked they would open themselves for his feast. He would be glad to tell Basket how good the food was in this new place, and hoped she would believe him. Right behind the driftwood, there was an unlimited supply of Biting Bush (Stinging Nettles) that his walking stick could knock down and his sling leather could strip off the leaves. He was eating like an Elder!

He pulled himself out of his comfortable shell into another overcast morning. His first glance was to the fire pit that showed signs of lingering coals. He placed some small firewood on the ashes and was happy to see a whisper of smoke. On the ring of stones, there were some of the small living stones that he had tried to cook. This morning they were partially open, a sign of their preparation. He scooped them out; perhaps he was eating too many, for the sweet flavor of the meat this morning had a sting to it. He wished he had one of Basket's corn cakes to go with them.

Tswa was refilling his water pouch at the stream when the first spasm attacked. He bent over with a groan. A second spasm caused him to look for a place to relieve his waste. He had violent runny waste. Another spasm made him gag and retch, as he was bent in pain. He vomited uncontrollably. He stumbled and would have fallen completely save for a big limb on a driftwood log. Staggering back toward the boat his intent was to lie down under his shelter, but another violent spasm shook him. Once again he could not control the explosion from both ends. More pain, more vomiting, more runs.

He had never been this violently ill. He staggered to his knees, tried to scramble into the only security he had, and as the darkness overwhelmed him, he slid into oblivion, swimming in a dark dream.

Meeting Klaw and Helps

As from a great distance, Tswa heard a woman's voice. Was it Basket, or his sister? A pleasant face came into focus. She was bathing his face and neck with a soft leather scrap scented sweetly of the forest. She was also speaking, but he could not understand her at all. A man leaned over her shoulder to stare at Tswa. He too murmured in a way that was unintelligible. For a moment Tswa was afraid that all his understanding had been drained along with all his stomach and bowel viscera.

He tried to rise and point across the big water, saying, "My name is 'Tswa,' son of Spear from the tribe Kwakiutl." That last word brought a grunt from his listeners. The man repeated "Kwakiutl."

Tswa collapsed back onto the elk robe, realizing how weak his body had become. There was much murmuring between the two, obviously about Tswa and his condition. The woman handed Tswa the leather bathing pad saying, "Glean self." Her expression was pleasant. Tswa realized simultaneously that she was trying to speak in his language, and he was naked as a baby. She had wiped his breeches and shirt with the sweet smelling liquid. The foul odor of sickness was lessening. Quickly he went about his bathing and dressing, but he still felt too weak to stand. The pair kept murmuring, and Tswa kept trying to understand them.

The man picked up the remaining small living rocks. Saying, "ba'..!" he threw them toward the water.

Understanding, Tswa repeated, "Bad!" He even made a grimace face to emphasize his understanding. The man nodded.

The woman offered Tswa the bottom of his big rock, now scrubbed clean and containing fresh water for him to drink. "Goon," she said softly.

Tswa responded, "Good water," and drank appreciatively. She smiled and was confident that their learning time was beginning, but not clear who was the student and who the teacher. One thing was clear, this young man would survive, and for that she was very glad.

They remained at the campsite for three more days. Tswa's only task apparently was to continue to clean his skin and clothes with the pleasant liquid from Helps' mixing pouch, a leather container that could rest on the cooking rock to blend the Juniper boughs, mint and water, and, of course, his challenge to learn and teach a mutual language.

Klaw disappeared for a morning hunt and returned with two rabbits and an arm-load of edible reeds. Each afternoon Helps went on a hunt for her own treasures. Happy Leaf (Mint) seemed to be her specialty, and she found another she called "Bright" (Lemon Balm.) When it was crushed and rubbed on the rabbit, Tswa was sure he had never eaten anything better.

The evenings seemed to be given to debate, although Tswa could not follow the subject. He would have been doubly interested if he had known they were arguing about his future. Klaw said he was strong enough to get here on his own, and now he was well enough to continue, on his own. They had considerable work to do yet for the tribe.

Helps lowered her eyes when she had a disagreement to voice. It was her opinion that since this was Salish land, he might become a slave sooner rather than later. Also, she felt that the Elders would be very interested in hearing about a fair place against the distant mountains that had good water and shelter, few villages, and abundant game to hunt.

"Then why don't we go into that new place and see for ourselves rather than bother the Elders?" Klaw was on the verge, but not quite angry with her, yet. He was still a bit critical of a young man who so foolishly consumed bad fish.

Helps carried the thought a bit further; "We can let them see through his eyes. They may have questions that we wouldn't think of. He already knows the way, and has left markers." She waited for him to say more, and when he didn't, she added, "Perhaps this is the story of our journey, to find him and bring him to the Elders."

Klaw was ready to say more, but fell quiet for quite some time. Finally, he said, "He must smell better to see the Elders."

She nodded in understanding and agreement, smiling at the ground. "We'll do better tomorrow."

By the third day Tswa was satisfied that the foul smell was gone. Helps said, "Almost" with a gracious smile. They were learning to speak more comfortably. She was older than his sister, but younger than Basket, and more attractive. Slowly, she had explained the plan of taking Tswa to the Elders. He had finally agreed when she told him that the Salish people, who controlled the land they were visiting, were very numerous, and hostile. If they found Tswa alone he would become a slave. The face she made left no doubt in his mind that it would be a very bad thing. "Each year," she told him, "they come to our village to steal."

"What do they take" he asked in surprise.

"Mostly women," she answered with a frown. "Sometimes children, or dogs," she looked into his eyes and shrugged, "food, slaves, anything they want." She gave a shudder of resignation, then murmured, "That why Elders let Helps come with Klaw on scout; no one to protect when he gone." Tswa was proud of her quick acquisition of Kwakiutl. She was doing much better at learning his language than he was at learning hers.

Klaw said from over her shoulder, "She too important to lose to Salish." Then before he would explain what he meant, he suggested that Tswa drag the hide boat back into the trees, and erect a marker pointing toward his home. That would serve two purposes. But it made Tswa a bit nervous to leave his only way of getting home. At least they should be able to find it again.

"How important is Helps," Tswa asked, a bit later. He wasn't sure if it was an appropriate question. If not, Klaw would let him know.

"She Shaman. Sit behind Chief in circle." Klaw was still. There was much more to say, but he wasn't about to do it. Tswa pondered on the meaning of a young woman carrying the title and authority of Shaman. It certainly elevated his appreciation for her efforts to communicate with him.

The next morning they rolled up their robes tightly and fashioned straps to carry them, along with their collecting bags. Each had a moderate burden, with Klaw carrying his bow and spear; Tswa his walking stick. Before they left, Klaw made sure to scatter the fire circle rocks and any sign they had been there. Tswa now understood how real the Salish danger was to their continued journey.

They walked single file near the tree-line; there was no conversation, just watchful eyes looking for any sign of trouble. When they came to a running stream, Tswa was quick to fill his water pouch. He noticed how carefully Klaw assisted Helps in the moving water. He treated her as though she might be fragile royalty. It made Tswa more aware of her status.

When the sun was overhead, they stopped to rest and eat. Miraculously, from her bag Helps produced cakes that were new to Tswa. As he munched, a large smile bloomed. "What kind of cake is this," he asked happily. "It is not corn cake."

Helps returned his smile of appreciation, saying, "Little Seed (Oat) cake with Tree Seeds (Hazelnut) ground with it." As she finished hers, she added, "Last longer in bag than corn cakes." The delight was still on Tswa's face.

They pushed on until twilight, when they ate more seed cakes and a strip of dried seal. There was no need for a fire. Stealth was their intent and they covered maximum distance doing it.

On the fourth day, when they stopped for their seed cake, Tswa heard the distinct call of geese from behind them. He hurried to his bag and drew out his sling, found a medium sized smooth stone, and looked at Klaw. "Is it food or trouble?" he asked.

Klaw shrugged with a crooked smile. "If you get, it food, no trouble." Once again Tswa was aware that his companions were answering in Kwakiutl. A line of geese came into sight, flying along the shoreline. Tswa tried to stay calm, remembering that he would need to throw well ahead of the moving target. As the sling swung over his head he exhaled, then released his stone.

He missed the bird he was aiming at, but to his surprise, and delight, the one following crumpled in mid flight and careened into the water. Helps was giggling, "Goo', Goo'!" Tswa ran toward the water, waded at first, and then swam to retrieve the large bird. When he proudly presented it to Klaw, he sniffed at his shirt. "Smell better?" he asked. The three chuckled as Klaw answered, "Smell goo'!" That night they had a fire so Helps could cook the strips of meat over the cooking stones. They would have food to spare for the rest of their journey.

The next morning Tswa was awakened by the quiet sounds of Klaw rolling up their sleeping robes, preparing to be on the way early. When he joined in the preparations, Klaw said quietly, "Must hurry now. Rain and big wind coming." Tswa was surprised that he had spoken in Haida. It must be urgent.

By noon they found the pile of rocks Klaw had left near the trees to indicate a new trail. Their journey must turn away from the shoreline and go west, toward an unknown village to Tswa, and a welcome he hoped might happen. They hurried on without taking time to eat.

The rain began mid-afternoon, before they had found a campsite. Klaw found a thicket that would give them some cover. It had a tree with a fork in it that would serve his purpose. While he cleared the ground on the storm side of the tree, he sent Tswa in search of three or four straight limbs to rest in the fork making a support for their shelter. The elk robe was pulled over the limbs, forming a cozy roof. Bows and limbs were added to protect them from the wind that Klaw insisted was on its way, and any passerby that might be following the same trail. He was so sure of the approaching storm that he dug a trench around their shelter. Now there was time to eat, and quietly talk, while the storm grew.

"Helps, can you tell me what are the plants you are hunting when you forage?" Tswa had finished a seed cake and two pieces of goose. He was afraid he might be overly talkative, especially now that he knew she was Shaman. But neither of the other two were saying anything, so Tswa tried to start a conversation. "I know that some is for food, but there is other."

For a bit, there was only the sound of the wind and rain as the storm built. Her voice was soft, almost like a song. "Your question is little, but the answer is very big." She considered how she would share with him such big secrets. "Klaw is a very good hunter, so I must also be good hunter for food. Our bodies are happy when we eat plenty of meat and plenty of plant, too. So I hunt plant to eat:" She held up her fingers as though keeping track. "Happy leaf, (Mint) Bright, (Lemon Balm) Biting Bush (Stinging Nettles) Little Seed, (Oats) Tree seeds (Filberts) Smoke, (Leeks) Happy, (Fern root) all these are goo' food, along with marsh reeds." She wondered if he would understand the next part.

"But also make body well when sick. Bleeder, (Milk Thistle) is good for wounds; Caps, (Echinacea) Dry Flower, (St. John's Wart) and Sacred Bark, (Cascara) also make body well." She stroked her abdomen, indicating the part of the body affected. "I give you Bleeder and Caps when you are sick with bad fish." She thought that information would bring more questions. It didn't. She continued, "If I find much of these, our village is happy, and no sick." She studied her listener's face carefully. When no further question was asked, she added, "I mix dried Seed Tree leaves with dried Biting Bush and fresh Happy leaf to make Circle's Smoke Pipe."

Tswa shook his head in confusion. "I don't understand 'Smoke Pipe'", he said with a puzzled frown. Actually, he didn't understand most of what she had just shared with him.

Suddenly Klaw held up his hand; four raised fingers indicated he was listening to four travelers passing nearby. All Tswa could hear was the wind in the trees and the pelting rain on their shelter. Klaw reached for an arrow and his bow. He closed his hand indicating the footsteps had stopped. The three in the shelter were on high alert, and silent. Several moments of intense listening crept by, the three not even daring to breathe. Finally, Klaw relaxed his hand, suggesting that the danger had passed. He gestured that they had continued on their way. But Tswa's heart was still beating rapidly. He was grateful that Klaw was so alert, and constantly on guard.

In the night, the storm passed as quickly as it had begun. Tswa was only aware of the stillness when he opened his eyes to a new dawn. Klaw and Helps were already rolling up their robes. It was time to continue their journey.

They trod single-file through the morning, resting only long enough to eat seed cakes and goose strips. Their camp site would once again be a cold one, for Klaw said he could smell smoke. They must be near a village or a hunting camp. Caution was necessary. In the gathering twilight, as they were spreading their sleeping robes, Helps asked Tswa, "Why you smile so big?" Her hand swooped in front of her face, reflecting a large grin.

"I have been talking to the wind today." He replied.

Klaw grunted in an obvious doubt, but Helps smiled warmly. "And does the wind talk back to you?" she wondered.

"Yes, if I pay attention. That is where I found the idea to leave my village, to take the boat. The wind whispered to me," Tswa replied.

"And did the wind talk to you today?" she asked in genuine interest.

"Yes," the lad answered

When he didn't go on, she asked, "Did the wind give you ideas today?"

Tswa's smile grew even larger. "Yes, but the wind has spoken in a mystery to me. It said that I learned many lessons yesterday, and if I listen, I will learn more lessons today." Then taking a breath, he went on, "And the wind said that if I listen more tomorrow, I will learn even more. The more I listen, the more I learn." He nodded his head.

"That is true," Helps agreed. "But why do you call it a mystery? Klaw is best listener I know, and the wisest man, too. He listens, and he learns."

"The smile had not diminished during their conversation. "But if I listen," Tswa asked, "And you listen, and Klaw always listens, who will teach the lessons?"

Klaw's voice was a rumble above a whisper, "Land teach. Lessons always before us. How many running streams have we crossed since the beach?" His gaze held Tswa. When no answer was given he said, "Seven streams. Means two more before we are at our village. The land teach us how far we must go." He rolled over into his robe, but left one more idea hovering in the air.

"Tomorrow you can teach Klaw how to throw stone with strap."

The wind had not been wrong, and Tswa's smile didn't fade until he fell asleep.

The first couple tries were humorous, but Tswa was careful to show no disrespect. "Place the stone in the pouch," he demonstrated again. "Then keep strap tight, swing around two, or three times." Once again he was trying to do it slowly enough for Klaw to follow. "Then release at target!" He released the short strap which sent the rock fairly accurately on its way. With a couple more tries Klaw had it working, and a couple more after that, Tswa was surprised at his proficiency. But then, Klaw was an outstanding hunter. A rare smile adorned Klaw's face. "You goo' teacher," was the only praise Tswa would get for his efforts. But it was quite enough.

With the new day, Tswa was more attentive to their path through the morning. They were, once again, in single-file, with Tswa at the rear. Occasionally he would see Helps' hand move to one side of the trail or the other. Always she was pointing at one of the plants she had mentioned. There was a Bright, in fact several. There was a Bleeder, and another. She pointed up to the fork of a large big leaf tree to a small fern that was growing in the moss. That was a Happy, and Tswa would not forget where to find that delightful root. It was a taste sensation he very much appreciated, but Helps had made it clear that if too much Happy was consumed, it gave a big stomach ache. And as they came to a dense thicket she pointed to a Sacred Bark; its power was in the bark, which had to be cut off in strips, then carefully dried, and finally ground with a smooth stone. The hot broth of it would either quiet a sick stomach, or loosen waste. Tswa thought he would use that with great care, and only rarely.

They crossed a running stream, and Tswa knew there was only one more to cross before they came to their village. He had many questions about what they would see, but no misgivings. Overhead he heard a sigh of breeze through the treetops, and once more found a warm smile. The wind was reminding him to listen, and learn.

Haida Village

It was late afternoon when the trail started a long descent. Tswa was tempted a time or two to run with ease down the hill. Suddenly they came through a tree line and before them was a large gathering of shelters, two or three times larger than the size of Tswa's village. It was situated on a shoulder of the hill, a large flat area before a steeper decline on the other side. Far in the distance, Tswa could see the reflection of the sun off a large water at least a day's journey away. Future explores would name that Port Alberni, and beyond it there were no mountains. They had crossed over what Tswa had called "the night mountains" where the sun went to sleep. He pondered where the sun might sleep tonight, and where he might as well.

As they entered the first line of shelters, Klaw said he would speak with Elders of the council. He turned toward shelters on the tree side of the village. Tswa continued to follow Helps, who was cheerfully greeted by nearly every shelter they passed. But when some of the more exuberant greeters came closer, they stopped in their tracks, aware of the foul smell of Tswa's clothes. Helps nodded, saying, "I think we must find you fresh clothes before you meet the council." They continued almost to the far side of the village, near the steep slope.

Helps stopped in front of a shelter, dropped her gathering bag and spread her hands before the door. "I come to you lodge, free of anger or fear. I embrace the peace and shelter you offer." She looked at Tswa, signaling him to follow her example of the open hands. "We are only an extension of our lodge," she said in flawless Kwakiutl. "If we corrupt our lodge with anger or fear, it is like spreading waste within it." Tswa nodded his understanding, and spread his hands in compliance. Tswa left his walking stick, elk robe and gathering bag beside the entrance.

Once inside there was a sparseness, and at the same time an elegance to the lodge. On the back wall there were several small gathering bags hanging neatly. He assumed they were filled with special plants she might need. There was a place for a small cooking fire, and robes spread out for sleeping. It was a lovely lodge.

"We must cleanse you completely before we can take you to the council." Helps spoke not with a sense of urgency, but as a matter of fact. "There is a neighbor whose son went fishing a year ago, and hasn't returned. She made him very nice pants and shirt. I think they will fit you."

"Do you think he will ever return?" Tswa felt that clean clothes would be marvelous, but he wasn't sure about wearing someone else's.

All Helps said as she left the room was, "It would be very nice."

She returned in only a few minutes, carrying a beautiful set of deer hide pants and shirt. There was elaborate stitching and fringe on the shirt. "Now you must bathe," she said, sounding every bit like a mother.

"There is a pond," she pointed a short distance away. "Go to the outlet, and scrub with Bright, especially your backside and legs. When you rinse," she showed him how to scoop the water with his hands, "make sure you are away from the pond. Do not fowl the water. That is very important to us, for our drinking and cooking water is dipped there. Is that clear?" The question was spoken softly, and Tswa knew it could have been much more direct."

"Yes, I understand," he answered as she gave him an armful of Bright leaves.

The pond was not difficult to find. It was a good sized lake and extended to the tree line. Tswa found the outlet, and followed the gentle flow a stone's throw from the pond. Bushes offered him a bit of privacy, and the smooth gravel rocks allowed him to kneel in the shallows and bath vigorously. He scrubbed as directed repeatedly, using all the Bright leaves until his skin was pink, and sweet smelling. He was even careful to wash his long hair. Certainly the bad smell was gone now.

After drying briefly in the sun and breeze, he pulled on the new clothes. He knew they were made for a young man, but not as young a Tswa. Their feel, however, made him seem taller, larger too. As he was about the return to Klaw's lodge, he noticed how uniform the stones were in the stream. They were about the size of an egg, smooth and white. He tucked several in the folds of his old clothes, thinking how happy he would be to show them to Basket, his mother, who kept her cycle for night play with such stones. It was the first he had thought of home in many days, and wondered briefly how long it would be before he saw them again.

From a distance, Klaw scarcely recognized the young man approaching his lodge, but the smile gave him away.

Klaw said, "Look like new man, taller, happier." Then, as Tswa got closer, Klaw tested the air and pronounced, "Smell good, too." Tswa was aware that Klaw had been working on his language skill as well.

He wasn't sure what he should do with his stained clothes, so he placed them in his gathering bag by the door. Then, remembering the words which Helps had spoken before going in, he spread his hands and said quietly, "I come to you lodge, free of anger or fear." He felt calm and at peace for the first time since his hide boat had left his mountain lake. From behind him Klaw nodded his approval, although Tswa didn't see it. In the lodge, Helps also smiled a warm approval, which Tswa did not see either.

The sun had set and still they sat around the cooking fire rocks. Klaw had explained that many of the men were on a summer hunt for deer and goat in the mountains to the north, which had high cliffs and rocky formations like giants. "Over half the council is gone," he said. "We must wait until their return to introduce a Kwakiutl." There seemed no other option but to patiently wait.

"One more word," he said softly as though there might be listeners in the gathering shadows, "Salish fellows have made some trouble on the rocky side of the village." He pointed briefly to the south side. "They steal food and an axe."

Helps asked, "How many are there?" Her face reflected both concern and disgust.

"Old Bear said he counted six. Maybe they are the same ones who passed by our shelter in the storm." It was perhaps the longest speech Tswa had heard from Klaw. But then he went on, "We need to be ready. They are young and foolish with greed."

Tswa confessed the activity of the day had left him very tired. He asked if he could spread his elk robe by the fire. He would like to place the deer hide shirt inside, however. There could still be a lingering smell in the robe.

Klaw whispered, "Best leave robe out where Salish will steal." Then with a chuckle, he added, "Then we can smell them coming long way."

Helps said Tswa could use their hunting robe; it was odor free. There was one thing they hadn't tried to get the waste smell completely gone. She suggested that they open the elk robe hair side down near the morning bushes, where they could urinate on it. "Maybe one will take away the other smell," she said optimistically. She then added that she had a sleeveless summer shirt that might fit him. "It will feel cool on this summer night." Once again Tswa was impressed with her language skill, and generosity. He moved his gathering bag away from the door to the lodge out of courtesy and spread the elk robe, perhaps for the last time.

For three days they waited. During that time Tswa was given hands-on lessons on plant gathering. Klaw was especially fond of Smokes, so they scoured the marshy area near the pond. Obviously others were also looking for them, for the green tubers were scarce. Tswa replaced the Bright he had used for bathing and a lot more. That one was easy to find, as was Happy Leaf. Helps finally had to tell him they had more than enough. And his willingness to harvest Biting Bush impressed her too. Tswa filled her cooking bag and had a pile for himself when she promised to make him a steamed pouch after supper soon.

Attack!

The memorable day began the morning of the fourth day. The three of them were sitting near the cooking fire when a scream came from the pond. A young girl was drawing water when she saw the Salish rise out of the bushes and head toward her. She shrieked and ran for home. Klaw ran for his bow, and for a frozen moment Tswa considered what he might do. Then he remembered his sling and the smooth stones. He had them in his hand along with his walking stick when Klaw came back out of the lodge. The line of Salish raiders was making its way up the hill, still about two bow-shots from the village.

Tswa launched a high arching shot, knowing that it was probably a wasted effort. But it might be a warning that turned them away. Before the first rock reached the ground, he launched a second. The first rock was short, of hitting the target squarely. Instead, it hit the first in line on the top of his foot, breaking two toes and cracking the bones of his foot. In a moaning whimper he fell to the ground. Before the second rock reached the ground, Tswa released yet another. The second rock hit the young Salish right in the middle of the face! His nose seemed to explode with a burst of blood. He too, fell whimpering on the ground. Now the remaining four raiders began to sprint toward the village. Tswa's third shot missed.

Tswa felt the thump of Klaw's hunting bow as he fired an arrow. The runner closest to him stumbled as the arrow went through his thigh. Tswa launched another rock directly at a young man who was now close enough for him to see his eyes and his twisted grimace. Klaw's bow thumped another shot and the next raider in line went down, also hit in the leg. Klaw was shooting to wound, not to kill. Tswa's rock hit the young man in the chest. He staggered and for a moment it seemed he, too, would crumple and fall. But he kept coming, a war axe in his hand. Tswa knew there was not enough time to sling another stone so he dropped his leather strap and picked up his walking stick. It was the closest thing to a weapon he could think of. The attacker was two steps from striking when the sharp point of the stick entered his chest, just below his shoulder. A look of shock spread across both their faces as Tswa thrust hard, and watched the point dig into the flesh, hit the shoulder bone, and then slide out the top of his shoulder, snapping the stick in half. The attacker screamed in pain, unable to move his arm, and fell to his knees in front of Tswa, who had the bulging top of the stick in his hand. Swinging it like a mallet, he cracked the wounded man on the side of his head, rendering him unconscious. The final runner skid to a stop as Klaw pointed a fully drawn arrow at his chest. "Take another step and you die," he growled, at the survivor who may not have understood the words, but had watched five of his comrade's fall in less than a minute. Immediately the young man fell on his face, pleading for mercy.

A number of men from the village came running to help in the defense. Unfortunately, that is about the same time the raider with the broken nose and bloody face chose to rise to his feet. He became an instant target for those who now had a passion for blood-letting. Tswa joined them as they ran at the staggering young man. The first one to reach him grabbed a hand-full of hair and yanked him backwards, a sharp blade ready to cut his throat. At the top of his lungs, Tswa screamed "No! Don't hurt him! He is my brother!" in the most perfect Haida he could muster.

The blade wielder paused just long enough for Tswa to throw his body as a shield over the former attacker. "He is my brother!"

A breathless Klaw interceded, and within a couple heartbeats had the noisy crowd under control. "Put away your weapons! Everything is under control! Look to the other five! Make sure they don't sneak away. No, this is not a Salish! He is my guest to speak to the council." There was a lot of shouting but those were the words of Klaw that brought order, especially when he mentioned the council.

The portion of Elders from the council not on the hunting trip, met a short distance from the crowd. It was their decision that the raiders should be taken to the Long House and kept securely bound until the next step could be chosen. Klaw found one of the round rocks Tswa had dropped. As they walked back to his lodge he tossed the stone in the air and caught it again, saying, "You listen to the wind good. Throw rock very far. Maybe I can listen too." Now that the trembling legs had stopped, Tswa felt elated. He thought it would be a good idea if he walked with the wind, and listened to what it might tell him.

The sun was setting when he returned to Klaw's lodge. He knew what they would want to talk about, but not sure how he could tell them what the wind had said. He found a bit of rabbit and corn cakes waiting for him. Helps had worried about Tswa's safety, but Klaw had only made a circle with his hand overhead, then smiled broadly. He had an almost parental joy in Tswa's performance during the attack. Tswa ate in silence, then drank gratefully from his water pouch.

Helps opened the discussion with a question. "What does the wind tell you to do with the Salish?" A gentle smile turned up the corner of her mouth, but he knew she wasn't teasing. Her gaze was steady and direct. "What punishment is proper for such rascals?"

Tswa was sure that she was baiting him, trying to get a prejudicial reaction from him.

"The wind told me," he began, sounding like a council member, "that this is a crucial fork in the path for the Haida and Salish people, maybe Kwakiutl too. One path leads to hostility and continued wars; and the other path leads to harmony and one coastal people, a strong tribe." His eyes were steady, first on Helps, then on Klaw. They thought he had an old soul, like speaking to an Elder returned from the past.

Klaw said, "Some want to cut their tendons," he made a sweeping motion behind his ankle, "and make them slaves."

Tswa nodded and asked, "Does the Haida need more cripples to serve them?"

Helps had not lost her curious smile. "What does the wind think we should do with them?"

From some recess of memory, Tswa pulled words that he had not heard, but that had been spoken over him, "If they were your sons, what would you want done with them?" Before either could answer he asked the second part of the memory, "Do you have so many sons that you can waste these?" He breathed in the twilight as though there might be power in the air. "I think you should tend their wounds as though they were your sons. Help them recover. Send the one who is well home, covered in berry juice as a sign of our intent." He had no idea what that meant, but it sounded fun. "Trade these young men for the women they have stolen. If the Salish come to do battle for them, make it clear that the first five to die will be these young warriors. If they come in peace, let there be a great meal, like a Potlatch. Free the men who may stay with the Haida, free the women who may choose to stay with the Salish. Wouldn't it be better to live as one family than stay in fear of raids?"

The Beginning of Understanding

The warrior part of Klaw resisted the logic, but the man nodded his head in agreement. Helps' smile only grew deeper in understanding.

With the dawn, Tswa made his way into the Long House, a place of village gatherings. He spread his hands before entering the community shelter, saying, "I come to you lodge, free of anger or fear. I embrace the peace and shelter you offer." The six captives were tied back to back, by their elbows, their hands bound in front of them. It was an uncomfortable way to secure them. Two guards were nearby with weapons, and fierce expressions. Tswa went first to the one with the broken toes; he placed a heavy stone about the size of his head, under the injured foot. Pressing the pad of the foot gently against the chilled stone from the pond, he said, "This will ease the ache." Of course no one understood him. He noted the urine puddles and deduced they had not had a chance to relieve themselves. Speaking clearly to them in Haida, he said, "I will loosen your ties. If you run, you will be crippled." He made the sign of chopping their tendon. No interpretation was necessary. One by one he untied them, and under the close watch of a guard, allowed them to go outside to relieve themselves. He had just established his concern for their dignity.

For the one whose nose had been broken, Tswa had a deer skin patch soaked in cold water. He could both clean his face, which was now swollen with a bright purple bruise; and he could comfort the pain of the fracture. The two who had suffered arrow wounds in their legs were given a clean patch to flush the wounds, and then a handful of crushed Bleeder, which would promote healing. He demonstrated how they should hold it firmly on their wounds. The shoulder wound was the most complicated for the walking stick had been removed none too gently; there was additional tearing of the wound. Once again Tswa offered a wet patch to cleanse it, then Bleeder to hold tightly to it,

When those chores were finished, Tswa offered them each a corn cake. When they were consumed and his water pouch had been drained, Tswa asked the guards to retie their bonds. Then Tswa squatted down near them and just looked deeply at each. The one with the broken nose was having trouble returning his gaze. He could remember how close he came to having his throat cut, but for the intervention of this strange young man. Tswa looked at the one with the shoulder injury, who had the axe aimed at him, again the long stare, and then a nod. Rising up, he said with conviction, "You are my brothers. The wind told me that is true." He turned and left the Long House, but he would return by mid-day and do it all again.

That routine continued for three more days. The captives began grunting appreciatively for Tswa's courtesy, but the guards were as sullen as ever. He noticed the shoulder wound was red and swollen, so he asked Helps to look at it. When she entered the Long

House the captives' attitudes became aggressive. Finally, Tswa shouted at them, "You are my brothers, now behave!" Curiously, they became quiet and accepted her attention, even though they didn't understand the words. Indeed, the shoulder wound needed more than Bleeder compresses. She was gone for just a moment, then returned with a small sharpened bone. She pressed the captive's face away, and gently lanced the wound, an issue of dark blood and fluid oozed out, captured by a wet patch. The young captive groaned from the pain, but did not flinch. "Now more Bleeder," she said appreciatively. "You are a Healer. Good." None of the other wounds seemed to need other treatment.

The next afternoon, the hunting party returned. They had been very successful so there was much meat to be distributed to each lodge. It had to be cut into strips and dried before it spoiled. For a few hours there was a unified effort throughout the village.

Klaw reported that the council would meet at sundown. Tswa was to be bathed and in the new deer skin shirt for the Long House gathering. Most of the village would be there. They could tell by the edge in his voice that Klaw was not certain how this meeting would be received. "Maybe we should talk to the wind before we go." Tswa was glad he was saying, "we."

The Council

Tswa felt as though he was being tried by the council instead to the Salish raiders. The large room was filled, with some women standing around the walls, then men sitting cross-legged around the council, who sat on hide robes in a circle around the captives. Pitch torches were lighted all around the large room. There was a lot of hushed murmuring, until the chief raised his talking stick. Silence filled the room.

"The ancestors were with us on the hunt, Chief Blade extolled, "and all went well. Once again Bear, Drum, Cloud and Axe were our marksmen and guides." A happy cheer was voiced. Once again the Chief held up the talking stick. "We will eat well through the harvest time. But now we must decide what to do with the captives that Klaw overwhelmed." Another cheer of appreciation, and once again up went the talking stick. The Chief offered it to Klaw, who in turn offered it to Helps, their Shaman.

Her voice was strong and clear enough to be heard in all corners of the room. "Tonight," she began, "the council will decide the fate of these men." She pointed at the captives who were now slumped in dejection.

"We can have them slain immediately." Those who had been victimized by the Salish murmured their approval. "We can cripple them and make them our slaves." There was more murmuring. She took a deep breath before saying, "Or we can treat them as our sons and use them to make a new nation with their people." The room was silent. "I think we can live as we always have, in fear of the larger Salish tribes, afraid for our women, our children, afraid that the stronger will be against us. But I also think that this night might be the birth of a new marriage between Haida and Salish, when we live not in fear but in peace." Many voices erupted in response, some in favor, many opposed. She raised the stick, and when the chatter continued, she banged the floor with the heel of the stick.

"Hear my suggestion to the council!" Her voice seemed to grow in force as she spoke with the authority of the Shaman. "Let us send one of the captives home with this proposal," she looked at Tswa before she continued. "We will exchange the six captives for the women the Salish have stolen from us. If they agree, these men can choose to return to their lodges, or stay here with us. The women will have the same choice; if they want to remain with their Salish men, they are free to do so." There was even louder discussion until she thumped the base of the stick again. "If the Salish come against us in war, these five will be the first to die. If the Salish come to us in peace, we will welcome them with a feast of peace, a Potlatch." The room fairly exploded with opinions, not many of them negative. For most, who had never experienced one, the thought of a Potlatch was only a wonderful dream. The captives in the center were also sensing the possibility of release for the first time.

They all sat a bit more erect. Helps gave the talking stick back to Klaw, who passed it immediately to the Chief.

The room was in pandemonium, with dozens of individual discussions, none of which were happening quietly. After a few minutes of the cacophony, the Chief began to restore order, thumping the base of the stick, more and more vigorously. Finally order was accomplished. Outside twilight was giving way to darkness, but inside, reason was overcoming hostility.

The Chief's voice was low and strong. "I have fought many battles." Those who were older remembered that his first young wife had been killed in a raid and his daughter stolen. "I have lost sons needlessly, and now words of peace are welcome to my ears. I can dream of a time when we could spend more time hunting and fishing, building strong lodges, than sharpening our blades and burying our dead. I would like to have my woman go into the bushes to pick berries without the threat of raiders. My house would be happier." There was a murmur of laughter, because the loud pitched and frequent arguments coming from the Chief's lodge were notorious. He concluded, "The council will think on these matters tonight, and agree in the morning. I will then meet the Kwakiutl." He shook his head as though clearing the shadows of confusion. "We went on a summer hunt, and suddenly our village has big decisions to make."

When they had returned to Klaw's lodge, Tswa was happy to see that there were still glowing coals in the cooking fire, and a cooking bag was hot on the cooking rocks. Helps paused to say directly to Tswa, "Thank you for giving me the words to speak to the council. They were the right words to cause them to think about choosing a new path." She poured a portion of steaming broth into a small drinking pouch, and gave it to Klaw, who seemed eager to receive it. Then she did the same thing for Tswa, who had no idea what a delight he was about to taste. She poured a small portion for herself, saying, "Sometimes I mix plant food for special taste." Tswa smelled a tantalizing aroma. "This is Biting Bush, Happy leaf and Dry Flower in hot water. You try it. It makes pleasant thoughts, like the wind." She sipped from her pouch. Klaw had almost finished his with a happy smile.

The flavor seemed to Tswa like sunshine, mountain air, and a meadow of flowers. He had never had anything so pleasant. The warmth spread down to his stomach and out to his fingertips. "Thank you Helps," he said, suddenly feeling the importance of the day. He had played a major role in the last two days, and his shoulders felt the heavy responsibility! "Thank you Klaw," he was feeling drowsy and more than ready for sleep. "May I put the deer shirt in the lodge?"

He was awake just as dawn was breaking, aware that this day was filled with possibilities. When he went into the lodge to get corn cakes, he found that Helps had put seven on the tray. Smiling, he understood that he would eat with the captives. "She must have listened to the wind," he thought. He hurried to the Long House to complete his chore and then get back to bathe and dress for the council. The guards had been more cordial, a fresh atmosphere of attitude. Even the captives could tell that there was a difference in the day. When they had all had an opportunity to relieve themselves, Tswa offered them a corn cake, taking the last one for himself. They were sitting cross-legged in a circle. Just before the guards retied their bonds, the one with the broken nose placed his hand gently on Tswa's shoulder and said something that sounded like, "Yume Hi Brod." Of course Tswa recognized the words so he placed his hand gently on the other's shoulder in return. Nodding, he said clearly, "You are my brother." They were speaking the same language, and for neither was it the one they had been taught as children.

Within a very short time the Long House was filled just as the night before. This time the Chief made it clear that only council members could speak. Any disrupters would be excluded. The village knew that the Chief was speaking the truth, because he found a satisfaction in ejecting folks from the meeting. It was a way of demonstrating his authority.

He reiterated the options for treating the raiders with justice, or mercy, and then asked for the council's thoughts. He began at his left, asking Klaw first.

"I was at first willing to take their lives. They came at us to steal or kill; it would be right to do the same. But I listened to the voice of reason that whispered there might be a better way for our village and people." He was silent, having said all that he needed to say.

One by one the council expressed pretty much the same conclusions. Only one wanted them made slaves, and the other speakers were sure it was because he was basically a lazy man, eager for someone else to do the work. As Tswa listened to each speaker he became more confident they could reach only one conclusion. He did wonder if the mention of a Potlatch was more important to them than a new day of justice. Twice he found Helps looking at him with that half-smile.

When the chief had heard from the council members, he turned to Helps, his Shaman. "Do you still believe it would be wise for us to reach out to our enemy this way?" She sensed that he was actually growing weary of his job and thinking like an old man instead of a wise leader.

"I do think this is the path of wisdom," Helps replied. "We have suffered in a way our children may not need to. They may look back at this day and applaud our courage." She really didn't need to say any more. The Elders were in unanimous agreement.

The Chief turned to Klaw. "You see to it! How many days to his village?" Klaw held up four fingers. "We will give them one day for their council, and one day for preparations and four days in return. If we do not see representatives from his village in ten days we will deal harshly with these." No one in the room doubted his intent. Several folks left, now that the main business was over. They weren't particularly interested in Klaw's guest.

When the Chief asked Tswa to step into the council ring, the young man again felt his legs tremble. He thought that Helps might have a plant to fix that. Klaw began a lengthy explanation of how they had come upon a sick young man who had eaten uncooked fish. The council groaned together. "We would have left him to recover but he identified himself as a Kwakiutl, who had crossed the big water in a very small craft. We decided that he might have information about the land on that side that might be useful for future decisions about our village." That was about all Klaw wanted to say and it was twice as much as Helps thought he would say. Apparently, Klaw had found affection for this young man.

The Chief asked Helps if she wanted to say anything more. She hesitated as though there was nothing more to say, but she had much they would hear.

"We were disgusted at first," she began. "We couldn't get the foul smell off his skin and clothes. We washed him but it didn't get him clean, then we made him walk behind." Several smiles were shared. "Then one day he took his leather strap and hurled a stone greater than a bow-shot and knocked a goose dead out of the air." Appreciative murmurs were exchanged. "He is a twelve year old healer; just look at the excellent care he has given these wounds." She walked among the captives. "I would not call him a warrior, but what would you call a man who can knock down three raiders just with stones, while a powerful bowman takes down the other three? He can hurl a stone twice as far as an arrow can fly. All that, and he talks to the wind." Now murmurs of disbelief fluttered about. "Like an Ancient One, he listens to the wind for advice, and then in obedience, he follows. He came to our land following the wisdom of the wind." She paced about as though searching for the next words. "I have no idea what he has to do with our story, or what we can learn from him, but I believe it would be a mistake to ignore him like a flock of passing birds." She felt spent as she returned to her place behind the Chief.

The room was perfectly still for a long moment. Everyone was trying to comprehend what they had just heard. "Could it be that this smelly stranger is an Ancient One come to guide them?"

Finally, the Chief asked Tswa if he could draw a picture of his journey from his home so they could ask him questions. Tswa thought that would be easy compared with the grilling he expected. He walked to the door and with a stick, drew a circle on the dirt floor. "My village is on a large lake with many fish. At night I intended to cross the lake in a small craft, but managed to find the outlet and began to float downstream. His stick made a wiggly line. "There were three slides and a falls." The stick made representative marks. "For three days I was in a river that grew when other streams joined," again his stick made lines showing the additions. "Then, for three more days I was in a very big water that was undrinkable. The water went one way for hours, then back the other way. That's when I learned to trust the wind. I held my elk robe for the wind to blow against and went faster than I could paddle. I stopped at every river that joined this big water to set another marker to show my way home." He made three more scratches in the dirt. "Finally, this water joined an even bigger one. I could see across it to mountains, but not right or left, it was so big. I had eaten my last strip of dried deer, so I trusted the wind. It blew for almost two days, and then I had to paddle the final half day." He went back to the beginning of his drawing, counting days, "Three days in the river, three days in the big water, three more crossing the biggest, and I was on the beach where Klaw found me. It took him four days to make me well enough to walk, five days up the beach," again his stick moved, "and three more to the village. I have been here for thirteen days, waiting to speak with you." The last sentence had a depth to it no one expected. There was a heavy pause.

The Chief asked, "How many villages did you see coming here?"

Tswa said, "This is the only one." A murmur of surprise skipped around the room.

"How many people did you see, hunters, or scouts?"

Tswa answered, "Only two: Klaw and Helps." There was a chuckle at his humor.

"Do you think you can find your way home village?"

"Of course," he replied. "I would never leave my family or home. It should only take me 17 days if the wind helps me. I left clear markers."

"What sort of hunting do you have?"

"My father, Spear, gets an elk every year and deer whenever we need it. There are goats in the higher hills and moose in the marshes below, red fish in the autumn, as much as we need. We never are in want."

"Are there many villages near yours?"

"I've never visited another, but Spear my father, is planning on the Potlatch soon, so there must be some." An appreciative murmur greeted the Potlatch reference.

"Where did you learn to speak Haida so well?"

"In the lodge of Klaw." There were no more questions as the villagers considered what had been accomplished in thirteen days.

The Chief finally said the council would speak more about this new information. He then asked Helps if the Smoking Pipe was prepared.

Yes," she replied boldly. "This is a happy time to make prayers." She placed a burning coal onto a ceremonial sort of thing with fringes and feathers and a hollow cup in which there was a dry substance. Presenting the Smoke Pipe to the Chief in a graceful gesture, she added, "a time to remember."

The Chief placed the small end of the pipe in his mouth and gave a puff. White smoke came from his mouth, to the amazement of a staring Tswa, and a mysterious aroma was a gift.

As Helps returned to her place behind the Chief, she whispered in Tswa's ear, "When it comes to you, do not let the smoke go deep, just a short puff, then blow it gently from your mouth. Do not cough; it is a sign of disrespect."

He watched the pipe pass from Elder to Elder, each with a white puff; there was more of the thick aroma. He would have enjoyed more information or a practice puff before it was his turn. His hand was trembling slightly as he received the pipe. He held it momentarily in front of his eyes, then slowly placed it to his mouth. "Just a short puff," she had advised, "Not too deep." Tswa pulled the smoke into his mouth, and as suddenly it escaped through his nose, two streams of white smoke. He did not cough, but with tears in his eyes, he passed the pipe to the Chief.

As the Elders were leaving the Long House, each had a different observation of Tswa's conduct, none of them negative; "Did you see the tears in his eyes? His heart is so big." "Did you see him salute us all with the pipe? He is humble." "He smoked as an Ancient One, through his nose." "I don't recall a more sacred pipe ceremony!" Tswa had to talk with the wind for hours before caring for his chore of captive treatment. It was late afternoon before he could return to the Long House.

Planned Peace

A member of the village had a Salish wife, who could act as an interpreter. Klaw spoke slowly so she could relay the information to the unwounded captive. "You tell your Chief to come in six days." The consequences had been graphically explained. He grasped the urgency of his task. A pouch with three corn cakes and three strips of dried seal was his food. They watched as he ran up the hill from the village and entered the tree-line without looking back. Now the waiting began.

Tswa revisited the stream below the pond to search for more of the white round stones. He brought ten of them back and formed them in a line by the fire. He was smiling broadly when he shared with Helps, "One will be taken away each day until the Salish return."

Since she could find no humor in his words to merit the big grin, she asked, "What is so entertaining about that?"

"I remember that Basket used stones to keep track of night play." He glanced at Helps to see her reaction to his reference.

Calmly, Helps asked, "Does she play with stones?"

Now nearly gleeful, Tswa said, "No, she wants no more children, so after her bleeding time, she sets out stones for Spear to see. When there are stones, night play is welcome between them. When the stones are gone, so is the play."

"And that prevents her from having more children?" Helps asked, now more interested.

"Must work, there are no more after me, and they still night play, some." Tswa answered, happy to be able to share information with her.

"But what happens if Spear wants night play and the rocks are gone?"

"I think that is why he is such a good swimmer in our lake," he replied, still with a happy grin.

The information was less humorous to Helps because she had wondered why she and Klaw had no children. "Perhaps," she thought, "this might be a clue. Klaw was interested in what Tswa called night play right after her bleeding time, then less interested as the days passed. Perhaps, if she put out the ten rocks as a sign of when they could begin night play…." It was worth a try. Her smile was less playful.

The days of sun light were still getting longer, with lingering twilight, but the waiting made them seem even longer. Each morning Tswa carried corn cakes to the Long House. Interest in the village had grown, and now several lodges were involved with providing corn cakes and strips of meat, some seal and most deer. There were two or three young women who were especially attentive as they helped these captives.

Tswa continued to speak to the five, trying to learn as much Salish as he could. When the interpreter joined the morning routine, interest spread even more, especially with the young women. The mood was so positive that the captives were allowed to be unfettered during the day, still with a dire threat if they should try to escape. In fact, they were as interested in the language classes as anyone else. The future of their tribe could be affected too.

One afternoon Klaw returned from a hunt with a ringtail (Raccoon), which would provide food for three or four days. The next day he went hunting for a new walking stick for Tswa. Patiently waiting was not in Klaw's nature.

The walking stick was most unusual. He had found a shoot growing from the base of a Seed Tree (Hazelnut), which was exceptionally straight, heavy and strong. When his axe separated the shoot, a portion of the root a bit larger than a clenched fist came with it. He had no way of knowing that the stick would be with Tswa for the rest of his life, occasionally as a talking stick, in emergencies as a weapon, and often as a scepter of authority. This day it was a shoot that needed to be peeled and dried, then perhaps shaped with a sharp stone. It was something to do before the Salish returned.

Tswa found a good use of his stained pants. With a steady hand he sliced it in long strips, from which he fashioned the now popular slings, for bird hunting and entertainment.

Helps presented an elk robe, now cleansed and practically dried from the repeated rinsing she had given it. Their experiment had worked surprisingly well. There was no trace of any foul odor. She would consider further the use of urine as a cleansing agent.

A conversation about fleas occurred one evening after corn cakes and deer strips. Tswa asked why they had none. He had realized on the first day in this village that fleas were absent. "In our village," he confessed, "they are so bad, we must often move the village."

Klaw chuckled at the needless effort. "This village has never moved. Same place, always."

"How is that possible?" Tswa asked in amazement. "They are everywhere."

Helps nodded. "But all problems have a solution if you can find it." Her eyes held Tswa's for a moment. "We burn away all grass from the lodges in the spring. We scatter," her hands made casting motions, "fine ashes from our cooking circles. Then the children are trained to find Bug Berry Tree (Elderberry) to pick the berries and leaves. We mash and grind to a pulp which is spread all around the village. No bugs, not even flying bugs," she made the tiny sign of a mosquito, "will come around our honored village."

Klaw added, "If the berry juice is rubbed on arms and legs, no bugs bite when we are hunting, and deer do not smell us."

"How can I recognize this Bug Berry Tree?" Tswa asked with great interest. If he could solve the problem of the fleas in his village he would be greater than the best in the trials.

"Easy," she replied. "Where there is Biting Bush there is Bug Berry nearby. They must like each other. I will show you." Her smile was genuine.

On the evening of the ninth day, a runner came down the hill toward the village. As he approached, he was recognized as the sixth captive, now bringing a message to the village. His chief and others from the Salish village, women and children too, were camped in the woods at the top. They would come down in the morning if they were welcome. After a drink of water and a corn cake, he was sent on his way back with a white feather, a sign of peace. The village began a hurried preparation to welcome the Salish with their finest clothes, and singing drums.

As usual, Tswa was awake with the dawn. When he had rolled his robe and taken care of morning duties, he looked into the lodge to find Helps with a tray of seed cakes made with sweet berries, and strips of dried seal. It would be a special breakfast for the captives still in the Long House. Helps also had a large quantity of Happy Leaf for them to bathe with before their village arrived. It was obvious that she wanted to show that her village had cared well for these young men.

When she and Tswa entered the Long House, there was a degree of cordiality. They knew the ordeal was coming to a good end. Helps offered them the food and leaves along with directions to the pond, and once again the caution to use only the running water. The young man with the broken nose was pretty well healed, except a green hue where the dark bruises had been. He stood and faced Tswa saying, "Name 'Sky,'" then, placing his hand on Tswa's shoulder he added, "my Brother." Tswa smiled warmly, returning the touch. "My Name is Tswa; you are my brother." He was pleased that they all could use Haida words when needed.

The Salish

The throb of Singing Drums announced the Salish. The Haida pressed toward the trail that led down the hill, the path their former foes would use. A festive sense of anticipation held the morning. And then they appeared; their Chief Otter, first in a berry red dyed robe, followed by his family. Then other Elders appeared, again, with their women and children. The drums set a happy song on the air. Slowly the procession, an envoy of perhaps thirty, made their way toward the village.

As they entered, they were joined by the Haida who were also dressed in their finest hides and robes. Smiles were everywhere. The convoy arrived at the Long House, where Chief Blade, wearing his prized white seal hide shirt and pants, greeted them. The Salish woman interpreted for him, adding courtesies and a far more gracious welcome than he had given. The guests would be given the use of the Long House and circle fire for cooking. After much gift giving and cordiality, the five young captives were presented, freshly bathed. Several young women were reunited with their families, a couple of them seeking affirmation to remain with their Salish men. It was an amazing beginning.

Tswa chose to watch from Klaw's lodge. He was not sure if his presence would complicate this peace-making moment, but he was sure that it was something the Haida and Salish should do together. Finally, he went to the pond to talk with the wind. He knew that the future of these two tribes would be changed. He had deep curiosity about his own.

While he was not in attendance at the gala gathering, Tswa was certainly the subject of conversations. Sky told his Chief how Tswa had used his own body as a shield to save Sky's life. Another conversation told how he talked with the wind, and crossed the big water. Finally in the mid afternoon, a group of both Haida and Salish men searched him out at the pond. They asked for a demonstration of the "throwing-strap." After some playful teasing, he agreed, if Klaw would get his hunting bow. Tswa found several smooth stones from the stream. Someone said, "I'll bet a corn cake he can't do it." Then another took the bet, and a third made a similar offer. By the time Klaw returned, the interest in their competition was heightened. Good natured speculation was going both ways.

Eventually Klaw raised his bow and with a thump, sent an arrow skyward. All eyes watched the arch of its flight and small splash about three quarters across the pond. The flint arrow tip was heavy enough to hold one end of the arrow under water, but the cedar shaft floated the feathers in clear sight. There were plenty of remarks that no rock could beat that distance. Even Tswa complimented Klaw for such a good shot.

Then he fit a stone and with three swings around his head, released a stone. Quickly he bent to pick up another, and in a blink had a second rock in flight before the first one hit the ground on the far side of the pond with a puff of dust. The eyes of all the men followed the arch of the second stone as it disappeared in the brush even farther than the first. Exclamations of surprise exploded. Both Klaw and Tswa smiled for they were not in the least surprised at the demonstration. They had seen it in action before.

In the spirit of Potlatch, Tswa presented "throwing straps" to Klaw, Chief Blade, the Salish Chief Otter, and his brother Sky. He was confident that very soon straps would be as common in the villages as his at home. It was the second time he had thought of his home. Suddenly there was an urge to return.

The dancing began before the evening meal and continued until dark, when several steaming cooking pouches were presented by the Haida women. Tswa was sure that he would never tire of the pleasant flavor or effect.

In the morning he missed the chore of caring for the captives. He stirred the ashes of the fresh cooking fire, waiting for Klaw to come out of his lodge. Tswa was sure there would be information of interest that the quiet man would share. Indeed he did. Klaw finally told him that the Salish would remain through this day, but leave for their own village in the morning. Two of the captives had asked if they could remain a while longer for they had met women of interest and negotiations were not complete.

"Their Chief told our Elders" he went on, "that they have family in a nearby village which has a hunting canoe they use for seals. Because of your bravery for their son, they will take you across the big water to the river near your home." Once again it was the longest speech he had heard from Klaw, and perhaps the most difficult to ponder.

Life here with Klaw and Helps was idyllic, but they were not his people, even though they had saved his life. He was not theirs. If he stayed with the Haida he would never be required to do trials. On the other hand, there very well might be a higher purpose in returning home and facing the judgment he had avoided. When Helps came out of the lodge her eyes were red and her face was puffy; she had been crying. Obviously it was a difficult topic for the day. Klaw said he must go hunting, and Helps said she needed to replenish the steaming pouch plants. Tswa smiled, "Appropriately, I will ponder this with the wind, on my own," he thought. By the time they returned, Tswa was sure of his decision.

The dancing began again in the afternoon. Again Tswa chose to remain at the lodge of Klaw, although there was little for him to do. He went to the pond stream and searched for more smooth white stones. He tried to explain his gratitude to Helps for all the information she had given him, and the fresh clothes she had found for him. He didn't understand why it seemed to make her cry more.

When Klaw returned he didn't have any fresh meat, but a walking stick that he had fashioned for Tswa. It was a bit longer than his old one, but much heavier and yet slimmer, not so cumbersome. A wooden shield had been carved to guard the sharp point. The root at the top was carved into the shape of a fist, partially closed. Klaw had found a white stone a little larger than the hollow space available. By pressure and tapping, he had forced the stone inside the finger shapes. As the wood dried, the stone would be held securely. "You are holding the heart of the Haida people," he said quietly. "Our hearts too." Before Tswa could say anything, the big man turned into his lodge and Helps was right behind him. Tswa stared at the treasure he had been given; then he understood why Helps was crying. He was too.

Even though Helps had prepared a steaming pouch, sleep was illusive for them all. They realized that however challenging the beginning of their short journey together might have been, this final night would be more trying. They had each found profound satisfaction together. When Klaw and Helps came out of the lodge into the dawn, they found Tswa had refreshed the cooking fire and rolled the robe ready for travel. Little was said; words were insufficient for this time.

Helps served seed cakes with berries, and strips of dried seal, then they were off to the Long House. Tswa silently promised to see this lodge again. At the Long House many were already gathered with the Salish. When the Elders from both tribes were in place, Chief Blade invited them to sit. He shared words of praise for the Salish people, their generosity, lovely women, and brave men. There were some who understood that the interpretation was much more elegant than his spoken words. A happy morning smile was shared and a genuine respect for the Salish interpreter. The Salish Chief Otter added their respect for such gracious hospitality and his appreciation for generosity never seen before. Once again, the interpretation was a gracious stretch of what was actually said. He concluded with an invitation to rejoin at this time next year to Potlatch in the Salish village. There was unanimous welcome for his words.

Chief Blade turned to Helps and asked if the Smoking Pipe was prepared. "Yes," she replied boldly. "This is a happy time to make prayers." She placed a burning coal onto the ceremonial pipe, and handed it to him, saying "a time to remember." The Chief drew in and released a cloud of fragrance. He handed the pipe to Chief Otter, who showed great respect. Tswa had been placed again at the right hand of Chief Blade so he watched the smoke device pass from hand to hand around the circle toward him. Once more he was trembling.

When the pipe came to him he accepted it as a tremendous honor. Carefully he raised the bowl to his eye level and looked at every Elder, Then taking the end between his lips he drew in a small puff of the warm flavor, and released it through his nose. He didn't cough! As he handed the sacred pipe to Chief Blade there were tears in his eyes, but not only from the smoke.

With one last round of exchanging gifts and embraces, the Salish Chief and Elders started up the hill as the farewells were concluding. Tswa and Sky had agreed to be at the back of the line, so they stepped to the side, which made it easy for Helps to find him and deliver a heartfelt kiss on his lips. Klaw simply patted his shoulder and made a circular hand motion over his head. Several others from the Haida came to touch or embrace him, or touch the walking stick, whose fame was beginning to spread already. A couple young women waited until everyone else had shared their parting, then giggling they kissed both Tswa and Sky before running back to the village.

Sky asked, "Do you always get this farewell?" His grin was still moist from the kisses.

Tswa said with an equally big smile, "Only in my dreams." They laughed as they both turned to follow the march into a new epoch of the story. It was two days before the second full moon since he had left Spear's lodge.

The Boat

The pace of the march was fast for the women and children, but slow for those in the back of the line. It gave Tswa ample time to search for special plants. Now that he knew what to look for, there was an abundance of Happy Leaf, and Bright. He had discovered several of Helps small collecting bags in his. She wanted to encourage him to find and collect useful plants. At one point, he noticed a fern growing in the fork of a big leaf tree. He dropped his walking stick, elk robe, and collecting bag to scramble up the tree, much to Sky's delight. Once back down, however, when he had scraped the skin off the root and broke it into two pieces, Sky's real delight was the strong sweet flavor of Happy. "Just nibble small pieces. If you eat too much you will get the runs." There was that mischievous smile again. They quickly caught up with the rest of the marchers. The day passed quickly with much conversation.

Sky explained that he was the oldest of four children born to Knapper and his woman, Moon. There was a little brother who was four summers old and two sisters. There had been two more sisters and a brother who had died at infancy. When Tswa replied that two brothers who had been born before him, had also died, Sky said simply, "I suppose we are the stronger ones." Indeed Tswa found in this young man a blend of strength and caring that was admirable.

Helps had said she put in enough cakes and deer strips for both of them. Each night as the Salish stopped for rest, Tswa and Sky found a place out of the way. They cold camped for convenience. On the fourth day they reached the Salish village. There was a brief conversation of the Elders and the decision was made that a smaller group of men would continue straight away for Nanoose Bay. This group of men were explorers; they would expect to be gone one moon, and if Sky wanted to accompany the group, he was given permission. They left immediately.

The pace of the next two days was much faster. There was no opportunity for harvesting, and both nights were cold camps. Tswa did notice several new plants and trees that he hoped he could see again. On the third day they came over the shoulder of a hill and stretching before them was a beautiful bay, beyond which Tswa could see the big water. Their pace quickened; it was mid day. By the time they approached the village, they were running. One of the men said, "The water is going down, we must hurry."

The village that they ran through seemed poorly organized or cared for. At the water's edge there was a group of men standing by a large cedar log that had been hollowed and shaped. Tswa assumed a messenger had preceded them. The sharp end of the boat was resting in the water; the remainder was resting on small round logs. Urgent commands were being given to join in the effort to launch the log boat. All began to push, and to Tswa's surprise, the craft moved. The more of it that got into the water, the easier it went. One of the original men jumped in with long leather straps. Another jumped in as well. Those at the front were holding onto the end of the straps, pulling it to a log that was supported by the shore. The task was finished; it was completely afloat. Now there was much shouting, both gratitude, and advice to leave. He and Sky were told to throw their bags and robes in the back. They would kneel on the robes while paddling. The urgency was that the water was going out. It would soon be too shallow to leave.

Tswa could tell that these men were accomplished at their tasks, like warriors going into battle. One by one they found their place in the front, each with a paddle on the alternating side. When the ninth one took his place he said that Sky would be number ten. As an afterthought Tswa was told to paddle when Sky could not continue. Then he was asked if he could find his way across the big water. Those in the front were already stroking hard with the paddles. Bit by bit the ten became synchronized, paddling with the leader; bit by bit the log picked up momentum. It was amazing! The sharp point on the front slid through the water like a powerful blade. Only when Tswa looked at the passing shoreline could he sense movement.

He saw them! The Morning Mountains were in sight and his mountain across the lake from the village. Clearly he knew the way home. But he also remembered how the water went one way, and then the other. If it was going out, he must advise them to compensate. He pointed slightly to the left. The leader shouted a command and those on the left side stopped paddling for three strokes. The nose of the boat turned slightly and Tswa pointed straight ahead. "Stay in that direction! It is right!" He felt like a bird flying over the water.

Time changed as the log boat sliced its way across the water. Now all that was heard was the grunt of the paddlers and the swish of the water rushing past. Grunt, swish, grunt, swish, it was like the boat's heartbeat. It was powerful; grunt, swish. Tswa was amazed at their progress. It had taken him three days to cross this. At this rate, they would be across before dark. Grunt, swish!

The sun was sliding into the highest part of the sky when the leader shouted a command and he, along with the second paddler, raised and boated their paddles. Quickly they drank from their pouches and consumed a seed cake. They rested for about ten more strokes, and then took up their paddles. On the next grunt, they pulled hard with their comrades. Two by two, that sequence gave the entire boat something to eat, a drink and a moment's rest. When finally it was Tswa and Sky's turn, as they ate Tswa asked if he should take a turn on the paddle.

"I am just starting," the lad with a crooked nose chuckled. "At the next rest, let's trade."

Tswa had been studying the shoreline in front of them. He was eager to see anything that looked familiar. At least he was convinced that making an allowance for the out-going water had brought them near a prominent point. Grunt, swish, grunt swish. Their effort was outstanding! There was still bright sunlight when he saw it! Pointing directly in front of the boat, he cried, "There's my marker. We are across the big water!" Now it would be easy to simply follow the shoreline to find the others. Grunt, swish! Sky saw the sun beginning to set behind his mountains for once. Tswa pointed to his markers as they were revealed. Grunt, swish. "We are in the river now," he announced, "the water is sweet again." Finally in the gathering twilight, he pointed to a marker high on the bank. "There is the first one I set. My village is within a day's walk up the hill." The leader guided their strokes to come to rest on the up side of the tributary. The nose of the boat slid in the sand for a moment, then it was still. One by one the weary men climbed off the point, taking their bag and robe with them. They relieved themselves, then dropped and slept right there. When talking about the performance of these men from Nanoose, for years to come, Tswa called them beyond human in their endurance and strength!

In the morning, surprisingly, the explorers were rested and ready to be on their way. They pulled the boat higher up the sand bar, and secured it with the long straps. Since they were no longer in the water that came and went; only a flood would wash it away. Their plan was to spend twelve suns exploring the area to the mossy side of the trees, and then twelve in the area to the dry side. They should be back at the boat by the summer full moon.

Sky assured them that he would rejoin them at that time. He would remain with Tswa until he was returned to his home. His Chief had made it clear that he would then fulfill his obligation to Tswa. Even though he argued that it was unnecessary, Tswa was happy to spend a few more days with his new brother.

The Real Trial

They set off following the stream through the thick brush until Tswa found a path made by the deer. It paralleled the stream but was open enough to see the way ahead. Sky noted that there were so many animals here they had made their own trail.

The sun was just coming over the Morning Mountains when they reached the waterfall. Tswa was surprised at the short drop of water, and remembered how his breath had been knocked out of him. "It was dark," he explained to Sky, "and it came upon me by surprise."

Sky was marveling at the beautiful meadow beside the stream. He said if he were choosing a place for a village, none could be more perfect than this one. It made Tswa smile with pride.

When they came to the first rapids Tswa realized how much quicker they were covering the distance than he had in his floating boat. He also remembered how Klaw had told him that the land teaches us. "There are only two more slides before we get to the lake and the village." He thought for a while about the older, stronger, young man who had chosen to walk second rather than lead. He knew that this place was as fresh to Tswa as it was to him, yet he deferred as if Tswa was the leader. What a strange person.

They stopped at the second slide to eat a seed cake. Once again Sky commented on the ideal location for a village with shelter against the hillside and open to the setting sun. He said that if he were choosing a place for a village, none could be more perfect than this one. Then he chuckled, knowing that Tswa was too.

Then Tswa turned to ask Sky, "Do you smell something bad? I think there is sickness on the air." Sky nodded in agreement. They left the lightness of humor behind as they pressed on.

As they reached the third slide, the stench was strong, and nearby. It was too much to be coming from a dead animal. A deep foreboding came over Tswa. He remembered vividly the moments of panic and pain he had suffered before losing consciousness. He had been alone and desperate. He was afraid for his village. They broke into a loping run to address the emergency.

Suddenly they came upon the silent lodges. Tswa was confused until he remembered Spear telling the family that the village was to be relocated. Now he stopped to orient himself, for none of these lodges looked familiar. He called out a greeting, but there was no answer. Like two ghosts they surveyed the two rows of buildings set in a half circle. When they reached the upper side Sky pointed to the problem; a black streak of dead grass emerging from the waste pit that went directly to the stream. It was upstream from the place the village would draw its water for cooking or drinking. They had poisoned themselves as he had by eating uncooked fish.

Sky shook his head. "They made terrible mistake," he said softly as though he might insult the designer. "Pit is not deep enough and in wrong place."

"Brother," Tswa said with tears in his eyes, "we must help them. Can you start a fire?" He looked around quickly assessing the available possibilities. He pointed away from the stream to another small meadow. "There, we can make them comfortable and safe." Sky nodded and began making a site. Tswa knew his task would be more grim. He had to find the people who were stricken.

From lodge to lodge he searched. These people had been sick for days. Some were not conscious, most were in a hazy dream state. Three were cold and lifeless, Spear's elderly uncle Hawk and his woman, Cloud. In a nearby lodge, the infant Star, who had been born in late winter, was also cold and lifeless. He found Spear and Basket not unconscious, but neither were they able to show signs of life. His sisters were under their robe breathing, but cold. He decided his first task would be to get them out into the sunshine, and then get some warm fluid in them.

Sky helped him carry the entire village out of their lodges and into the meadow. If their robes were not completely soiled, they laid the men and women on them. A small ring of stones encircled the fire, with cooking stones that would heat pouches. Tswa used most of the small bag of dried Caps he had along with his Happy Leaf. It would be a slow task, but he was determined to accomplish it. While he began administering the steaming liquid, a small drinking pouch at a time, Sky continued to carry the still forms. The afternoon sun was high and warm when they stopped to assess the problem again. Some of the villagers were showing signs of stirring, some were retching, but most were just lying quietly in misery. Basket had recognized Tswa and squeezed his hand. She was making no effort to get up, however. Tswa made another round with the cup, dispensing a sip at a time, as they could swallow it. After a while Sky made a round of offering clean water from their pouches.

"We have some seed cakes," Sky suggested. "Perhaps we could give a small portion for them to have something to digest."

Tswa nodded. "It is a big task, like climbing a mountain."

"But, like crossing the big water, we can do it one stroke at a time." A wry grin played on the face of this great friend.

At that inappropriate moment, a group of three young men came down the trail from the lake. Camas, Tswa's brother, was in the lead. They had been on an eight day hunt, and had nothing to show for it. He strode into the cluster of prone villagers like a conquering hero. "What is this all about?" His question had the aroma of ignorance. "Tswa, what are you up to?" He stepped forward and clubbed Tswa on the side of his head, knocking him to his knees.

Immediately, Sky jumped up growling, "Do not hit Thunder! He is my Shaman!" The words were spoken in Salish, which of course sounded like babbling.

"This little coward ran away from the trials?" the older brother sneered. "Who are you Bent Nose to stand in my way?" He raised his hand to strike again, but Sky's foot was faster. The kick caught Camas just under the ribs. His face went white, then dusty as he fell into the dirt. One of the others took a stride forward only to be met by the sharpened end of Tswa's walking stick, poked in his chest just under his chin. Not a word was spoken but Tswa just shook his head. Finally, Tswa said,

"There is more sickness in this place than I can care for. You have two options, help or leave."

The one on the end of the walking stick was still bold enough to challenge the younger man. "And if I want to do neither?"

Tswa gave a sudden thrust of the stick, just enough to break the skin and cause a trickle of blood to ooze onto his chest. "Then I will care for your wounds when I get these others well." Camas tried to stand, but couldn't, and fell backwards on his rump.

"Take all the corn cakes you have," Tswa commanded, "place a portion in each mouth. They are awake enough to chew and swallow it." The three, Camas bent over and favoring his side, scurried away to do as they were bid. Tswa looked at Sky and said, "Thank you. I have wanted to do that for a long time. He deserves worse." Now that there were five of them helping, the task would go more quickly. By sunset there were good signs of recovery. Tswa had made more steaming pouches, this time with Biting Bush and Happy Leaf. He encouraged people to continue to rest and grow stronger. His heart was happy when he noticed Basket helping his sisters with a steaming pouch. Eventually, darkness embraced the scene. The fire was banked with extra wood in the hopes that it would hold all night.

Sleep was again fitful for Tswa, however. He kept envisioning his sick village, and listening again to the echo of Sky calling him "Thunder." With the dawn Tswa scoured the swampy area around the marsh by the lake. He found three Smokes, enough for steaming pouches. When it was hot, he also added Bleeder, and had eager recipients. All the folks were improved, many to the point of walking back to their lodges. Even Spear was leaning on his elbow, not quite strong enough to stand, but well enough to no longer be prone. Basket was sitting cross-legged beside him.

Tirelessly, Sky and Tswa had worked through the morning, serving those who as yet did not realize the cause of their distress. Finally, in a voice that could be heard by all, he said, "Listen friends, the sickness was in your water, because once again the waste pit was placed wrong, and dug wrong. It has poisoned the stream. Do not drink or bathe here. Do not eat anything that was cooked with this water. We will cover this mistake with dirt. The lake is clean. The Chief will speak with the Elders." That last part could get him in trouble he knew, but sooner or later Chief Bear would speak with them. All in all he was satisfied with his first public address to his village.

With all the healing that was going on Tswa knew that he had to apologize to Spear for running off before the trial. It seemed the perfect time to do it now, while Spear was still weakened by the poison.

"May I speak with you, father?" he asked. After a moment, which seemed extra long to the son, Spear nodded and invited him to sit on his robe.

"I must apologize for any embarrassment I caused you. I was afraid I could not bring you honor, and so I brought dishonor to myself. In time I will tell you how two moons have changed me forever. Today I ask that you consider what I did for our village and weigh that against what I did that displeased you. I am deeply sorry." He sat quietly, with his head down. Anyone who cared to look could see a contrite young man before his father.

Finally Spear murmured, "Can you teach Basket how to make Steaming Cup in the mornings?" Obviously, Spear had forgiven him.

"Thank you father," Tswa replied with sincerity. "I think you should have the Elders meet immediately to repair the stream, and choose a new site for the village, My friend Sky can suggest how the waste pit should be dug, and where. In their village, they never have to move because of the waste pit." He hoped that Spear would hear the offer and not see in it impertinence. "And he can drive away the fleas, too!" Tswa would Helps with that part.

He decided to take one more inspection of the villagers who seemed to be coming back to life. He told Sky that he would share their last deer strip, and then he would walk with the wind for a while.

The sun was high overhead when Tswa returned. He found the little meadow, their emergency lodge, empty except for rolled robes and the smoldering ashes of the cooking fire. Sky was dozing on the collecting bags which had been fairly emptied.

"I'm glad you are back. I think the Council is meeting, perhaps with everyone. They understand the need to move, even if they are still weakened. I have repaired the waste pit." His steady gaze held a satisfaction of service.

"Shall we join them," Tswa asked. "We can share our wisdom." He chuckled at the humor of a young man unwilling to face the trials, and a Salish, who no one could understand, having wisdom to share. As it turned out they actually did.

When they arrived at the Chief's lodge, nearly all the village was gathered. Opinions were being voiced, some loudly. Tswa was surprised how limited most of the people were. Their life had, for the most part, been spent on the shore of the lake. Their desire was to return there, to a fresh place. Few people had ever been downstream, and a different few had hunted up in the mountains.

Spear gazed at Tswa for just a moment, weighing the possibility of saving face for his son. "Tswa has been on a journey for two moons," he offered. "Perhaps he can tell us what he saw." The faces of the village swung toward this strange lad with a big stick and a friend that spoke gibberish.

"I floated down the stream all night and a day," he began. Some heads shook in disbelief. "I rode down the river as it grew toward the bad water. I crossed the big water for three days and when I was out of food, I ate uncooked fish and became as sick as you were. People of the Haida found me and made me well. They took me to their lodge until I was strong. There was a Potlatch with the Salish people who sent me home with one of their sons as a guide. I came back across the big water in a hunting canoe. Two days ago, we followed the stream from the river back here where we found you all sick." He looked at his father expecting questions, but the crowd was still. Even Camas was looking at Tswa with wonder. "The reason you don't understand what Sky is saying is that we only know Kwakiutl, our little language. There are so many others."

"But did you see any village sites that might be good for us?" Spear sounded as though he were speaking to another adult instead of his son.

Tswa turned to Sky and interpreted the question in Salish. Smiling with understanding, Sky held up two fingers, and rattled off words that everyone was eager to hear.

"He says," Tswa began, "there are two that would make every other village envious. One is about an hour's walk from here. It has a huge meadow for crops and Potlatch." There was the magic word again. "The other is a little farther, about two hour's walk. It has a smaller meadow, but still ample room for crops or Potlatch, and a waterfall that would be so full of red fish in the fall you could pick them out by hand. That one is also closer to open water where you could hunt for seals, as well as deer and elk."

Sky rattled off another long sentence. Immediately the faces turned back to Tswa for translation. "Sky wants you to know that he will lead a group of Elders or hunters who would like to see these places so you can make a fair choice. He also said it is not a difficult journey, downhill most of the way, coming back it is just a little uphill." Laughter responded to the guest who was endearing himself to them all.

Tswa explained that Sky could lead the party by himself. When Sky responded that Tswa was needed to translate. "You can teach them Salish on the trip." They would return in just the second day. "Besides," Tswa added, "I have a very important task to do in those two days.

Early the next morning six of the Kwakiutls and Sky started on a journey of discovery. Tswa waved them on their way, and then turned to his project. He had found a wonderful piece of big leaf (Maple) tree that had surrendered a flawless piece of straight grain wood about the size of his hand. With his small sharp blade, he began carving a hole a bit off center; slowly one tiny fleck at a time, the bowl appeared. It looked right to him. It took the entire morning before he could say he was satisfied. Then he began on the side, doing the same thing. His hands were weary, and there were three or four small nicks that bled. Into the evening he continued to remove tiny pieces of wood from the outside of the chunk until the shape of a beautiful eagle's head was evident.

The next morning he addressed the big leaf fresh branch about as long as his arm. He removed the bark from it, and then carefully scored from one end to the other a straight line. With his blade he went over and over that line until he reached the spongy pulp center. Remembering how Helps had used a sharpened bird bone to lance the wound, he found and sharpened the perfect tool. With only a little pressure he could spread the cut wide enough to remove the pulp. He scraped until he was satisfied with the tube of the pipe. When he fit the branch securely onto the eagle's head, he was pleased; the smoke pipe was going to work. He wrapped the stem with a band of leather, so the smoke would draw properly and not spill out. Then he bound it securely with a leather thong, and a white feather was fit onto the loose end as a fitting adornment.

Sky and the elders returned by mid afternoon, full of excitement. They had liked both sites and were anxious for the council to discuss them. The evening was noisy but positive. It was a matter of choosing the better of two wonderful options. The vote was finally taken and the nearer of the two, the one by the second rapids, was chosen, the logic being that they would be more sheltered and could still easily fish below the falls. Preparations to move would begin in the morning.

Chief Bear was about to adjourn the evening when Tswa asked, "This is a happy time for prayer. Would the Chief like a sacred pipe for remembrance?"

The startled Chief answered, "We have no Shaman."

"You do now. I am Shaman of the First Nation." Tswa said slowly. "The Salish has given me the name 'Thunder', for I speak with the wind." His father could only stare at him in surprise. Camas, on the other hand, could only shake his head with a scowl. Angrily he turned and left the gathering, adding to the growing darkness.

Each answer gave the Chief another question to ask. "We have no sacred pipe." His face was twisted in the puzzle.

Thunder reached behind him into his collection bag and drew out a magnificent pipe, already filled with a mixture of crushed Seed Tree leaves, Biting Bush and fresh Happy Leaves, just as he had been instructed. A warm murmur escaped from the council. "I have shared the Sacred Smoke with the Haida and the Salish. Tonight, now with the Kwakiutl, we complete the circle; we are one nation, the First Nation, with many villages, families as numerous as the stars in a summer sky. We are brothers." He asked Sky to fetch a burning coal from the cooking fire.

When Sky returned, he placed the coal on the filled bowl, and would have returned to the back seat, but Thunder caught his sleeve and pulled him down on his right side. "This is a happy time to make prayers," Thunder raised the pipe to his eyes and gazed briefly at each man in the circle. Presenting the Smoke Pipe to the Chief in a graceful gesture, he added, "a time to remember." Chief Bear, whose hands were trembling, accepted the pipe as though it might be fragile. He puffed once then twice, and rich white smoke came from his mouth. He smiled joyously, and passed the pipe to his left.

Thunder leaned into Sky and whispered softly, "Take a small puff; do not breathe deeply. Puff it out of your mouth, and do not cough. That is a discourtesy." He gave a playful nudge with his shoulder.

The pipe came to Sky who lifted it to his eyes and looked at the Chief. Truly this was a historic moment, he thought, "a time to remember." He puffed softly and released the smoke with no cough. He passed the pipe to Thunder, who raised it and said to the council, "You are my brothers." He drew in a puff of smoke and released it through his nose. Once again his eyes were burning as he returned the pipe to the Chief.

None of the council wanted to leave the circle until the Chief announced that plot selection in the new location would be on a first come basis, rather than selection by status. Now they were motivated to begin packing,

As Sky and Thunder were walking away, Sky asked, "If I were to remain longer than the full moon, so I could help your family move, do you think I could teach your sister Carry to speak Salish?"

Finis: Book one, A Walk With the Wind

Assorted Legends

The name "Thunder" became very popular in the First Nation villages, usually attached to talented Shaman. One such, describes the Shaman of the Tlingit's, who in winter wore a heavy black robe, the hide of a bear he had killed with his walking stick.

The people of the Kwakiutl claim that Thunder was their Shaman for many generations. He had a lodge with them but no family. He would disappear to walk with the wind for seasons at a time.

The people of the First Nation who spoke Salish and Haida claim they had a powerful Shaman who talked with the wind, and warned them when trouble was near. They also claimed he had a lodge in their village, with a large family...... in both.

A story is told that a Shaman named "Helps" was stolen by the Heiltsuk because of her lasting beauty. She warned the chief that if he slept with her one night, his hair would fall out. If he slept with her two nights, his manhood would fall off. On the second day, a bald chief sent her home with many gifts of apology.

A legend is told about the powerful chief of the Haida named "Klaw", who had four sons in his old age. It is said that two of them chose to cross the big water to start new villages in the fertile fields and valleys near the Morning Mountains.

Book 2

Feast in the Dirt

Table of Contents

A Lodge for Thunder

Spear considered the request for a day and a night before he answered. "Yes, Tswa, or Thunder, you may claim Hawk's lodge, if no one else related wants it. You are second generation family; but there might be others. I'll ask." There was little actual value in the structure; the worth was in the establishment of a man's lodge. Spear could not remember a time when a twelve year old man had his own lodge, without a woman. But nothing about Thunder seemed predictable. He would be surprised if any other in the family wanted to deal with the old lodge frame.

Thunder had helped carry the frail bodies of Hawk and Cloud to the sacred ground, where a shallow grave was scraped. They looked small in the dirt, but when they were covered with the dirt and then stones, a quiet dignity held the hillside. Spear had said simply, "That is how we have buried our dead since this village began."

It made Spear smile when he reflected on how hard Sky and Thunder had worked to move his lodge. They had been tireless, even working harder than Basket. It had dawned on the father finally, that Sky might have intentions on Carry, his daughter. "Yes, he is a strong worker," he thought happily. He was also aware that Camas, his older son, had not helped at all with any of the relocation to the new site. Sky had shown himself to be a real leader, even choosing three sites for waste pits. He also helped burn the grass away from the village site, promising that it was the first step in ridding the fleas, forever. "Yes, he is a strong worker for our village," Spear thought with satisfaction.

Hawk's lodge was the last one standing in the old site. Spear had told Thunder that when the village residents learned that their new Shaman would have it as his own, a sense of pride had even protected the robes and belongings left by Hawk and his woman.

"Tell me again why you want a lodge away from the others in your village," Sky asked, still confused.

"It seems to me that higher on the hillside gives more visibility of the whole area, and more sunset light, too," Thunder answered. "On top of that I have no woman who wants neighbors to talk with, or children at play. This seems like a fine place to talk with the wind." He had a wide smile as he added, "And if I am wrong, we can move it down with the rest."

They had spent three long days digging into the side hill to make a level site. With a sharpened pole, they had loosened the soil of the back wall, then scooping it onto an old robe, they had moved the dirt to the front edge and slid it off. Only when Sky saw the eventual finished site could he ask, "Is this going to be your Long House?"

"It sort of makes sense, doesn't it?" Thunder replied. "They didn't have a Shaman, and now they do; they didn't have a Long House, and now..." He left it unfinished. Sky wondered why Thunder had said "they" instead of "we."

The task of moving Hawk's lodge was more inconvenient than difficult. The dismantling was easy, organizing the robes, skins, and gathering bags took some time. The discovery of three cooking pouches made Thunder eager for an evening fire, and drinking pouches of Biting Bush with Happy Leaf. They could have the entire lodge moved in three trips, and finished by tomorrow evening.

Lost a Brother,
Gained an Adversary

The first part was moving the frame, which were basically poles held together with cedar fiber cord. They were careful to save every bit for reconstruction. That part took a full day, and brought a satisfied sigh when the skeletal frame was finished. They admired their labor, and could easily see how dramatic the finished lodge would be. It would take two trips to move the robes that made up the roof and sides.

When they returned with the first heavy load of robes, Sky cried out, "Something has torn it all apart!" The frame, instead of neat and ready to be covered, was lying in disarray, not one pole attached to another. When the two disappointed builders took a closer look, they found moccasin tracks in the fresh dirt.

"Camas," Thunder growled. "No one else is stupid enough to do this."

Sky asked, "Is he stupid enough to try to take the other robes?" Both men were already moving back toward the old village site, running now with urgency. Thunder had his walking stick, Sky would find a club of sorts; there were no other weapons available. Not a word was spoken between them, just the heavy breathing of exertion.

They burst upon Camas and his two villainous friends as they were throwing the robes and bags into the stream. The one nearest to Sky lifted a club and stepped into a swing. Sky instantly dropped onto his right side and kicked as hard as he could on the exposed and rigid knee. There was a sickening snap and a scream that startled the other two, who had been focused on the destruction of the lodge material. Both swung around instantly. Unfortunately for Camas, that was the moment of Thunder's walking stick striking at what would have been his shoulder, and turned out to be the side of his face. The heavy fist-like stick, carrying a stone, tore a wound never intended. He dropped to his knees spitting blood and teeth. The third culprit did the smart thing. Once before he had felt the point of Thunder's walking stick; he surrendered, holding his hands out submissively.

"You," Thunder ordered him, "retrieve all the robes! Lose one and I will knock out your teeth as well!" There was no discussion, the young man bounded into the stream, gathering their intended insult, and placing them safely on the shore. He did an exceptional job, for he had never seen anyone wounded as drastically as Camas, whose face was torn from the corner of his mouth to his ear. He would wear that scar for the rest of his life.

Thunder squatted in front of Camas. Their eyes held onto one another, one with caring, and the other with fury. Thunder said, "I cannot understand what made you do this. I meant you no harm, yet you know it is against our law to destroy another man's lodge. We are brothers, and yet you have made us enemies. Did I do something to you?" The only answer was an intense glare. Thunder decided to leave the robes where they lay, and take the three to Spear, who would take them to Chief Bear, after Basket tried to bind their wounds.

The stern faces of the council reflected the troubled minds. They had never had to make a decision like this. Camas was the son of Spear, a prominent council member, as were the other two who had aided in the destruction, sons of council members. There was some discussion about the possibility of cause, but the facts were pretty clear. Without provocation, the three had rampaged the new lodge of Thunder, and the choices were limited. The three could be crippled and made slaves, or they could be banished from the village. The latter choice allowed them to seek a full life for themselves; but it would never be in this village. A unanimous vote chose the latter. Hearts were broken in at least three lodges. Two other fathers offered to help Spear remake the frame of Thunder's lodge. It was a sad time, but the law.

Romance

From the village, Thunder's lodge, perched up on the side of the hill, looked like any other. But when Thunder's family came to inspect the final results of their work, it became instantly clear that this was no ordinary village lodge; it had been extended to more than twice its original length. Before he invited them to enter, he paused, extended his hands palms up saying, "I come to you lodge, free of anger or fear. I embrace the peace and shelter you offer." He told them that a very wise Shaman of the Haida instructed him to cleanse himself in this way before entering his lodge. He invited his family to follow the example of the open hands. "We are only an extension of our lodge," he said, remembering Helps' words. "If we corrupt our lodge with anger or fear, it is like spreading waste within it." There was an awkward moment as the family dealt with the unusual leadership of the youngest. Finally, Spear opened his hands, and entered.

"It is very large," Basket noted, "Enough for two families."

"Who will clean this big place?" Carry, his older sister asked.

Thoughtfully, Spear noted, "This looks more like a Long House than a lodge."

"That was my thought also," Sky replied brightly. They looked closely at Thunder.

The young Shaman said, "It is eight days before the summer full moon, the time when the explorers will be back at the big canoe. Sky may go back to his Salish village with them. I thought I might also." When his family looked at him with a start, he held up his hand. "But," he continued, "I don't like being on the far side of the big water from home; I know that Sky feels the same way. So our paths may part." There was stillness.

"I have also thought there is much to see and learn if I explore the dry side of the trees (south) from our village. If I missed a Potlatch it only means there are many villages to visit. So if I think of this as my lodge, it will only be so occasionally. The rest of the time I will walk with the wind." When no one had a comment, he added, "It would be a comfortable place for the council to meet."

Sky said, "It is large enough for two families." He caught Basket's smile, "We have eight days to talk about this. But tonight Thunder has prepared a special cooking pouch for us." Again he caught Basket's smile and wondered if there might be more unspoken delight.

Thunder poured a drinking pouch half full of steaming Caps and Happy Leaf liquid. He presented it to Spear. "This was a delightful lesson from the Haida. I think of Klaw and Helps whenever I taste it." He poured another for Sky and then for Basket, Carry, and Spring, his other sister. Finally he lifted another for himself saying, "This makes my heart feel light, but not as much as you do." He sipped the warm liquid and sensed it's magic.

The next morning Sky had to walk through the village three times before he found Carry. She had seen him on the second time through, but had stayed out of sight. She was trembling with excitement when she tried to casually ask, "Is my little brother with you?"

Sky was grateful for the Kwakiutl he had learned from Thunder. He replied, "I think he is talking with the wind, trying to see what the future has in store."

"Does he do that often?" She really didn't want to talk about Tswa. Oh, it was so hard to understand how he had such a large name now. Before Sky could answer, she added, "We are so very proud of how much you have helped our village. We might have died without your care."

Now it was Sky's turn to search for the correct words. He thought talking about Thunder was easier than being honored by this delightfully lovely girl. "In less than three moons he has turned my life upside down." That seemed neutral enough. "Did you know," pointing to his deformed nose, "he gave this to me?"

"No," she said in genuine surprise, "he's not a fighter. You must have tripped over his unconscious body." Her laughter was like a melody on the morning.

The smile stayed on his face as Sky told her, "Six of us Salish were attacking a Haida village. Thunder dropped three of us with his sling and his walking stick. A warrior bowman wounded two of the others. They stopped us before we could even get near the village."

Carry was shaking her head, "Is this really true? My father would be shocked to hear it." She had taken a step nearer Sky as if searching for the story.

"It is very true, and then, he cared for our injuries until we were well. The part that I still think about is that his stone only knocked me senseless for a moment.

I staggered to my feet." Sky shifted his feet as though remembering the moment, "A Haida villager grabbed my hair and was about to cut my throat when Thunder threw himself between me and the blade, shouting that we were brothers." His head was shaking, still finding it hard to believe. "Have you ever heard of such a heroic thing?"

Carry gently placed her hand on Sky's chest. "That is not the young brother I thought I knew. He must have great love for you."

Sky was having trouble thinking of anything except the feather-light touch and the warmth of her hand. "I'd like to think I was blessed at that moment. I think, however, that his heart is more courageous than we can imagine." He placed his hand on hers for just a moment, to remember the touch.

The next day Spear found Sky in the village and asked him if he would mind showing them the falls again. Carry wanted to see a waterfall, and Basket was excited to go too. Maybe Thunder could join them? That didn't happen, but the four of them had a delightful outing, complete with seed and berry cakes and strips of dried deer.

The following day it was a trip to the lake. Sky had the impression that they liked him because he had helped them move. While he wasn't clear about that, he knew he was very fond of their daughter, Carry, and grateful that he could converse with them. He wondered if this had been in Thunder's plan all along.

The Wind Knows
Your Way Home

"I understand, it is a difficult problem," Thunder said. "You would like to remain with Carry, and you desire to see Knapper's lodge again. They are the family of your story."

A distraught Sky spoke quietly, "But perhaps my story is to be here with the Kwakiutl. This feels like my lodge too."

"The summer full moon will be in three days," Thunder said thoughtfully. "The explorers will return across the big water. Perhaps we should talk with the wind as we go to join them. In three days we will know the path we must follow. The wind knows your way home." Thunder thought it best to speak with assurance, even though his heart was wrestling with the same issues. "Perhaps we should leave now, and make a camp at the boat. I would like to inform Spear of our journey. Is there someone you would like to tell as well?"

A light rain began as they were on the downhill trail, and the wind was perfectly calm. "Thunder, is the wind not speaking to you or has it gone to another lodge?" Sky tried to give cheer to a day that had not been very

~ 101 ~

happy. It was hard to part from someone as pleasant as Carry.

"Perhaps," Thunder answered, "it is a problem so big to solve that the wind must consider it alone before giving us a path." They had only a short distance to go before they would see the boat. Thunder hoped the explorers would be there waiting. Perhaps they would have welcome information that could help.

When they arrived at the boat, the explorers had more than information. They had a young man who was apparently lost. They reported that the land they had visited on the mossy side of the trees (North) was unpopulated, although there was abundant water and game. They had found several ideal sites for a village. They had then crossed the river and found a very tall mountain, which they spent a day climbing and from which they could see three villages near the big water, and perhaps a smaller fishing camp too. When they returned with the log boat, they had found this young man who seemed very troubled. "He speaks Salish, but not well. He said he was going fishing, although he has nothing to use to catch fish. He was not sure of his path, and got lost in the fog. He cried when we first arrived, but after eating a piece of seal, he has just sat there looking sad."

Thunder went over to the dejected fellow, who was at least a head taller, and more muscular. "Hello, my name is Thunder. I live up the hill. Is your lodge close by?" He waited for an answer that didn't come. In Salish he asked, "Are you a fisherman?"

The young man's face turned toward Thunder with a look of recognition. "I can't fish, and I can't find my lodge." A look of grief was in his eyes.

"My name is Thunder," he said in Salish, "What's yours?"

They call me Slow Bear, but my father named me Bear." His head rose a bit with the interest.

"Did you come here in the canoe?" It seemed like an obvious question, but perhaps it would get him to talk more.

"I tried to go to the little island. Somehow the rain and the fog confused me again." He looked damp and quite uncomfortable.

Thunder asked, "Is this your canoe?"

The sad head first nodded, then after reconsideration, shook. "No. It was my grandfather's, but he died."

"Do you live in your father's lodge?" Thunder was aware of a deep puzzle.

"No, everyone died but me. I live in the lodge alone." There was a reason to be sad.

Thunder returned to the cluster of men standing by the boat. He was quiet for a moment, until he realized they were waiting for him to speak. "I believe," he began, looking at Sky, "that the wind wants me to help this fellow find his home. I know there are no islands on this side of the river, so he must have come from over there." He pointed to the south side. "Sky, I think our path must part here. I wanted to return to the Haida village, but I do feel that the wind wants me to do this more." His face reflected his sorrow.

"Perhaps not," Sky interjected. "I have just told these folks that I do not feel that I have fulfilled my obligation to you. I have asked them to tell my lodge that I will stay here until the next summer full moon. Perhaps they will join me here. Perhaps I will have a lodge here by then. Only the wind knows." His confident smile was contagious. "Can the canoe hold three?"

The explorers said they had an old spare paddle that would help the canoe. They also shared six strips of seal. Just that quickly a new path opened.

"We know there is no island downstream from here," Thunder said, trying to make a plan for Slow Bear's return. "So let's follow the far shore until we find one." He was not sure if the strategy was sound, but it seemed like an only option. Looking at Slow Bear's sad face, Thunder smiled and said, "Don't worry, the wind knows your way home." Sky was in the back with a paddle, Slow Bear in the middle, also paddling, and Thunder looking for some sign that might be familiar to Slow Bear.

They had gone about an hour when Thunder realized that they were no longer going against the current. They were on another branch of the river. Apparently they had gone around the top of a large island. He suggested that they see if there was a shoreline directly ahead of them. In another hour they found the island that Slow Bear recognized, and only in a short while more, he pointed to a cove, which was his home.

The entire village, at least a dozen lodges, was ghostlike still, and more than a little terrifying. Slow Bear explained that it had started in late winter with a cough that seemed to hit everyone at the same time. He had suffered for days, but then his went away. For the others, there was fever, then convulsions. "And then they died, cold," Slow Bear explained. "I took them out of the cove and let the water have them." Finally, he was the only survivor.

They were walking past a row of empty lodges when Slow Bear asked, "What happened to these?" Three shelters were in disarray, flattened and scattered. "They were not like this when I went fishing this morning." With a closer look, they found moccasin prints, fresh and familiar.

"It couldn't be them," Sky murmured.

"It couldn't be anyone else," Thunder answered angrily. "There must be a trail from our village to here. They didn't have a canoe." Turning to Slow Bear, Thunder asked, "How close is the nearest village?"

He pointed south saying, "I don't know, maybe a half day. I've never been there."

Another Encounter

"Slow Bear," Sky wondered, "do you have enough to eat here? Do you need our help?"

"Food is no problem," he answered. "People had much corn and dried fish, some deer strips. I collect it all when they were gone. There is much left. Would you like some?" His offer was genuine if somewhat less than gracious.

"We have plenty," Thunder said. "But could we use a couple sleeping robes. We might need some shelter for a couple of days.

"Just take any. They don't belong to me. They belong to the air." He smiled at his own humor.

In the morning they had followed the moccasin tracks to an overgrown but useable trail. They were heading south, too. After a while Sky asked, "What do you suppose will happen to all those hides and robes?" He was thinking about an entire village slowly rotting. "Do you think any of it is usable?"

Thunder replied, "I've been thinking the same question, but about Slow Bear. I doubt if he can make it another season alone. Do you think he is usable?" They walked in silence for a time before Thunder continued,

"I think you could easily collect enough robes to make a lodge for yourself, and maybe for someone else, too."

They could smell and see smoke rising ahead of them, and knew they were approaching a large village. The trail broke through the low brush and Sky and Thunder found themselves confronted by six angry warriors. Thunder said clearly in Haida, "I am Thunder, Shaman of the First Nation. I greet you in peace."

The nearest warrior was less than impressed with the greeting. "Are you with the scar-face one, and the cripple?" He held a sizable club ready for action.

Thunder continued to speak for Sky also. "We are not with them. This man gave him the limp, and I gave the other a scar with this walking stick. But there was a third one with them."

The attitude of the guardians relaxed, ever so slightly. "What do you want here, holy man?" one of the six asked, less than cordially.

"I am here to heal their wounds, and yours." Thunder thought he might as well jump right into it, even if that wasn't their plan. "These men are Kwakiutl. I know their village. They have been cast out for destroying another's lodge."

One of the six explained that the three had tried to steal women. "They had subdued one when several of the villagers converged on them," he said slowly. "There was a terrible fight; several were wounded seriously. Finally the three had been bludgeoned unconscious, taken to the Long House where they were secured. Chief Storm Cloud and the council are deciding their fate at this moment." It was said as fact with little emotion.

"Will you take me to the council that I might speak to them?" Thunder was hoping that he might hear from the wind soon.

A silent procession wound through the lodges to the Long House, where Thunder was ushered before the council.

"I greet you on behalf of the First Nation," he said boldly, "a joining of the Haida, Salish and Kwakiutl."

A voice speaking Haida said, "That's the first I've heard of a joining! Who are you?"

"I am Thunder, named Shaman by the Salish," he answered in Haida. "I smoked the pipe with Chief Blade of the Haida, and Chief Otter of the Salish, and Chief Bear of the Kwakiutl."

"And what do you seek here with the Sechelt?" another voice asked in Salish.

Speaking just as easily in Salish, Thunder answered, "I came to help heal the hurts these men have caused." His eyes were fixed on the three slumped forms in captivity.

"If we have chosen to kill them will you still try to heal them?" A wry murmur punctuated the idea.

"If killing them is your choice, I doubt if it will heal your hurts. I would then look to aid your villagers who were wounded in your defense." Thunder's voice was calm, his tone matter of fact.

"What other choice do we have but to kill them for a crime like this?"

"There are always choices," Thunder smiled. "You could just let them go, banished from your village forever. The Kwakiutl tried that and it only sent them here to you." He paused as though thinking of other punishments. "You could cripple them and turn them into slaves, but who needs more of those?" Then, as though it had just occurred to him, he said, "You could take them in a canoe to an island remote enough to hold them forever. What justice! They came seeking women, let them live a lifetime without any. You have many choices to consider." When there was no other comment, he asked, "If you will tell me where to find your wounded; I will do all in my power to bring them comfort."

As Thunder was guided by one of the villagers, he asked Sky to take a robe back out near the village entrance. As they came in he had noticed five or six Bleeders. "Be careful, they have piercing fingers. We will probably use them all." The rest of the day was spent assessing, cleansing wounds, and applying pads of crushed Bleeder and Biting Bush. "How could three attackers make this much damage?" he asked himself. There were three wounds, all in the back of their victims, that were deep and troublesome. Thunder tried to flush them clean with water and apply the healing pads, but the bleeding persisted. As the sun was setting, he made his way back to the Long House. He had been told of the council's decision and wanted to speak to Camas once more.

As he approached the huddled three, he asked if he could care for their wounds. Camas nearly screamed, "Leave us Whelp! We don't need your care, or your Salish woman's!" Thunder squatted beside them, silent, trying to understand the depth of insult to Sky and himself. In the shadows, he looked at the angry scar deforming his brother's face.

"Camas, brother," Thunder said quietly, "I have pleaded for our village to treat you with mercy, and I have pleaded for your life from the Sechelt. I cannot plead more. Tomorrow they will take you by canoe to an island where you will be without food, shelter or tools. It seems to me that you have bigger worries than me or Sky, who only wanted to help you." The glaring eyes were eloquent in their fury. "I will tell Basket that we spoke of her in this final meeting." He rose to leave, having nothing further to say.

"It is not our final meeting," Camas hissed. "I will see you again when I take your life from you." He violently twisted against the straps that held him tightly.

It took four days before Thunder could feel confident that the back wounds would heal. He had made a lance from a thin branch from the Peeling Bark tree (Madrona). The smooth hard wood could be sharpened enough to open and drain the wounds of the collected black blood and fluid. When the fever set in, he added ground Cap as a paste with the Bleeder, and blended it in water for them to drink. He was grateful for the lessons he had been given by watching Helps. It seemed like long ago. Finally he was confident they could be on their way to assist Slow Bear.

Future Abundance

"You need not go," Chief Storm Cloud was speaking to them. "You could make a lodge here. There are many who would welcome you, some very handsome young women." His smile was genuine.

"But you already have a Shaman," Thunder answered with an equal smile.

"He is good for sacred pipe, and singing drums, but he never gets his hands bloody." It was the highest compliment the Chief could shape for Thunder and the most public criticism he could direct at an absent holy man.

Becoming more serious, Thunder explained, "The wind has guided me to Slow Bear, the only survivor at the fishing camp. I do not believe he could survive another season alone, nor do I think he could be a part of your village. He would have already tried that. I think we will make him a Kwakiutl, and get him to grow corn for us. We usually run out before summer."

"Do you know about the three sisters?" the Chief asked, still with a grin.

Thunder chuckled, "I'm only twelve years old, and Sky is going to take my sister as his woman if we get back to the village before anything else happens." Sky gave a shocked expression that Thunder could so casually mention that possibility.

"No, I'm only teasing you," the Chief continued. "At Potlatch last year, coastal people from the south brought us the gift of seeds. The three sisters are corn, beans and squash! We had never seen such plants. The squash are like great colored stones that may be kept through the winter. When the flesh is baked over the fire it is much better than cakes. The beans can be eaten fresh, or dried and kept through winter also. When they are cooked in a pouch they crush into a wonderful paste on cakes. For your service to our village, let me see if there are any lodges that have some seeds to spare."

When the pair left the Sechelt village, they carried a gathering bag heavily weighted with seeds that promised a new future for a young man, who as yet didn't understand the changes about to happen to him. They also had a supply of seed cakes and strips of dried deer that would more than feed them on the way home. There had been ample instructions for planting and tending the potential crops, and accumulating fresh seeds. It would be a new day for the Kwakiutl village as well.

The Chief had never mentioned the three canoes that had delivered condemned men to separate islands, to meet their individual fate.

Sky and Thunder were back in the deserted village before the sun was overhead. They found Slow Bear straddling a log, absorbed in making a pattern on it with a sharp blade. When Sky studied the pattern more closely he recognized it. "Slow Bear are you making a bear on the log?"

The happy face looked at Sky with appreciation. "My grandfather said it was our totem. We are bear people; people of the bear," he corrected himself. I didn't do all of this; my grandfather started it. There are many in that pile," he pointed to a brush covered stack of logs.

Thunder asked, "Slow Bear, would you like to take your totem to our Chief? You know, his name is Bear; just like you." Then answering a question that wasn't asked, he said, "Yes. We can go by canoe and then walk; or we could find the trail that the bad people who knocked down the lodges used when they came here." Without pausing for any conversation, he continued, "Yes, you can come back to your lodge if you would like to, or we can move it to the Kwakiutl village where you would be a welcome guest. We could even bring some of the robes from the other lodges and build new ones. Would you like that?" Overhead a breeze rustled the trees.

"But I wouldn't know…" he left it unspoken. "I'd be alone," Slow Bear said sadly.

Thunder said, "Not as alone as you are here. You only have memories here, and you can take those with you. Look! You already know two of us, and before three nights, you will know," he held up his fingers, "this many more. Then you can invite the children to your fire in the evening and tell them the stories your grandfather told you." Thunder looked at the troubled face. It was a lot of information to get all at once, especially if your name was Slow Bear.

"I've saved the best for the last," Thunder said with a flare. "We don't have a chief grower in our village, someone who can plant and nurture our big garden, where our new plants are going to feed the village. Slow Bear, you can be that person." Sky looked around suddenly as a strong puff of wind moved his hair. He glanced at Thunder.

Slow Bear looked into Thunder's eyes deeply. "Are you trying to fool me? I don't like that game." He looked at Sky. "Can I truly be a chief.... What did he call it?"

Sky nearly laughed, "If Thunder says it will happen," Sky ruffled the young man's hair, "it will happen. You can bet on it. You can be our chief grower! That means our very first one!" Thunder did not miss the use of "our grower." There was considerable conversation, but the decision had already been made, and Slow Bear was growing more enthused about the change with every new thought. They decided to spend one day taking inventory of the village, which included the discovery of a log canoe, the sort the explorers had used. That could be of tremendous value. Then they packed Slow Bear's personal items, which were of little value. They thought it might be easier, carrying a load of hides and robes, to follow the trail back up the hill than take the canoe. If Thunder was right, it might be a quicker journey, and once used, an easy return for the abandoned items.

He was right. The faint trail, probably made by deer originally, ambled through a gentle valley. Within a couple hours the trail led them up a long slope. When they topped a small ridge, he could smell smoke from cooking fires before he could hear the tumbling water. Soon he identified the sound of the rapids. A few more minutes, working their way through the tangle of brush, they came out directly across from their village. As they were fording the knee-deep water above the rapids, Sky said, "I think there will be many who make that trip tomorrow. And now that we know the Sechelt village is only a half day farther, there will be some who adventure there as well."

Their first stop was the lodge of Spear. Thunder wanted to introduce Slow Bear and ask for Spear's thoughts on a council meeting to discuss an organized food patch. Sky, on the other hand, wanted to see Carry, and share with her his plans to stay in the village. Perhaps he would even build a new lodge, if the council would allow it.

"I know one council member who would like that very much," she said with a sparkle in her eye.

Spear agreed to request a meeting with Chief Bear. "If you add a steaming pouch at the conclusion, I am sure he will be in favor of the meeting." He raised his eyebrows in a playful question, "In the Long House?"

"Of course," his son answered. "What is such a fine Long House for but to make important decisions?" They both silently wondered if this was the same young man who just three moons ago refused the trials.

The Council's Approval

The afternoon was given to sweeping the outside and inside of the lodge with a fir bough. Thunder opened the smoke vent so they could have a small fire inside. Around that circle, they spread all the robes they had, including the four they had brought from Slow Bear's village. They gathered more than enough wood for a cooking fire outside, that would keep the cooking rocks hot. When they had filled two cooking pouches with stream water and added abundant portions of Cap and Biting Bush, and Happy Leaf, they were satisfied that the preparations were complete.

The sun was still well above the distant mountains when Carry came up the hill with the announcement that the council would eat their evening meal and come up for the meeting. She said with a happy smile, "Even Chief Bear will be here with the seven Elders. He rarely attends. You must have special news." Thunder joined in the smile as he noticed that her gaze was directed more at Sky than towards him.

"I think we are prepared." Thunder said quietly. "Most of our news is very good."

As expected, Spear was the first to make his way up to the lodge, but the rest must have been watching, for they gathered immediately, each carrying a drinking pouch in anticipation. There was surprise when they realized the size of the shelter, and good natured bantering that it had taken the wisdom of a youth to provide it. The village was already in evening shadows of the trees, but the sunlight bathed the interior of this lodge, with its opening facing the distant mountains. The setting was as perfect as any could remember. The council was seated; Thunder stood at the lodge opening, and Sky, with Slow Bear, stood outside, by the cooking fire where the cooking pouches were already heating, the aroma of Caps and Biting Bush heavy in the air. The Chief began by asking Spear to tell the council the series of events that had brought them together again.

"Some of this will be news to me as well," he began. Our friend Sky had bid us farewell and was on his way back across the big water to his Salish home. The wind told Tswa, who is now known as Thunder, that a young man in distress needed help finding his home on the water. Sky made the decision to remain with them to fulfill a battle obligation to Thunder." With those words there was a murmur as the council exchanged wondering glances. Spear said, "Why don't I let Thunder explain the rest?" The Chief beckoned Thunder to join them. When he was seated beside his father, the Chief asked for an explanation of a battle obligation.

"I was staying at the lodge of Klaw, an excellent Haida hunter," Thunder began, "when six Salish warriors came at the Haida village. I threw three stones with my sling, as fast as I could. The first one was short, but hit a warrior on the foot, breaking bones. He fell to fight no more. The bowman was shooting to wound, not to kill. He dropped a second; then my second stone hit Sky in the face. Stunned, he fell also. The bowman dropped another attacker and I cast a stone point blank that hit another in his chest, but he only stumbled and kept coming at me with an axe. My last defense was my walking stick with the sharpened tip. I jabbed that in his shoulder before he could swing the ax. It pierced his flesh and came out the top. He couldn't move his arm and when he fell he broke the stick. The sixth attacker surrendered when he saw that the bowman was prepared to take his life."

Pausing to catch his breath, Thunder continued. "The village men were arriving, wanting some of the fight, just as Sky staggered to his feet with his bloody face. One of the men pulled him down by his hair, prepared to cut his throat. I spoke enough Haida to scream that he was my brother. It gave me enough time to place my body as a shield for him. Then I tended their wounds until the Salish Chief came to make peace with a Potlatch." The council was breathless. "He thinks I saved his life, but I think I broke his handsome nose. I'm not sure who has the obligation." Outside a sigh of wind stirred the air while the brilliant sunset illuminated the inside of the lodge, and the faces of those who listened in amazement.

"You know how helpful Sky has been in first healing, and then relocating our village. When we thought it was time for him to rejoin the Salish explorers across the big water, he chose to help me take a confused young man back to his home on the other side of the river. When we found his village we learned that all of the people, eleven lodges, had died last winter from a coughing sickness. Only Slow Bear survived. He has been living alone all this time."

"He discovered that while he had been gone, someone had knocked down three lodges; their moccasins tracks left little doubt who it might be. Sky and I followed the trail for over half a day and came to the village of the Sechelt." Now interested or concerned comments were shared. When they quieted, Thunder went on. "Three men, one with a limp, and one with a scarred face, had tried to steal women. A terrible fight had injured many; three stabbed in the back were near death." More comments were murmured. "The three were captured and were being sentenced to death when I arrived. I pleaded mercy for them, and finally the council decided to take them by canoe to uninhabited islands, without food, shelter or tools. It might have been a death sentence of a different sort." The council was silent, lost in the possibilities of his account. "Or," he added quietly, "depending on their training and fortitude, it may have been an opportunity to survive." Several nodded in hope. The sunset had disappeared behind the mountains and twilight was fading. Sky brought wood to freshen the fire.

"Now the happy news," Thunder said quietly, trying to change the mood. "Sky and I attended the wounded; even the severely hurt were finally healed. In gratitude the Chief had the people share spare seeds with us of the Three Sisters." When snickers were loud enough to stop him, Thunder said, "It confused me too. The Three Sisters are corn, which they call Maize, beans, which is food that grows on vines, and squash which are large orange rock-looking fruit that are better than cakes. We were given enough seeds to feed our village forever, if we have someone who will tend the plants." Faces looked from one to another; it sounded like a job no one wanted.

"The wind whispered to me two days ago. We had helped a young man find his lodge, but it was no place to live. He is Slow Bear." Thunder said the words extra slowly, communicating a condition without causing a loss of dignity. "He is willing to make his lodge with us, which might take some oversight, which I or Sky will gladly do. If we allow him to have a lodge with us, and offer him some of the meat we hunt, he will be our grower. He will learn to cultivate, plant, and tend the growth of enough food to share with every lodge." A positive murmur was shared. "And speaking of lodges, there are ten lodges plus Slow Bear's just half a morning's walk from here, with very many robes and hides and sharp blades and cooking pouches that we can have for the moving. There is a log canoe for seal hunting and a smaller hide canoe for fishing. His grandfather was teaching him how to carve bear totems. If we are willing to bring them we could mark the trail into our village, and one for the Chief's lodge." He was sure he had suggested too much.

Thunder gave a happy smile, concluding, "Tonight the council could give permission for both Sky and Slow Bear to have lodges in our village. May I introduce them to you?" Now conversation was unchecked, as the two men were presented. There were so many things to consider, the closeness of other villages never before visited, robes, new food, and two new lodges. Spear's smile was marred only by the thoughts of his son, Camas. Finally the Chief called for a vote to add two new lodges to their village. "Palms up for adding." He may have been thinking about the steaming pouches. A unanimous vote welcomed two new male members to the village, and a host of possibilities too.

Sky brought in the steaming cooking pouch and Thunder dipped a drinking pouch for the chief, and then he went around the circle. Each empty drinking pouch was filled and emptied with satisfaction. Finally, one by one the men of the council made their way down the hill to their own lodges. They couldn't recall a more informative and motivating gathering. Thunder had changed their future.

Salvage and a New Start

In the morning, Sky had barely taken care of morning relief when Carry came up the hill. She said radiantly, "There are several who would like you to guide us to the abandoned village." The transition was happening faster than they expected.

Thunder asked Slow Bear if he would like to return with them. "Can we bring the canoe, and catching basket?" the young man wondered. "Soon the red fish will be here. And we will need the drying racks, too."

"I don't know what a catching basket is," Thunder said with a puzzled expression.

"It's a large hard basket that you drag behind canoe. Lift the fish out easy." Slow Bear was glad to have information that was useful to Thunder.

Before the sun was above the Morning Mountains, a stream of nearly twenty villagers were on their way down through the meadow valley to the abandoned lodges. Beyond the advantage of new hides and robes, this journey made the path to their neighbors more definite. It would be used often in the future.

Once in the still lodges folks began gathering everything that might be useful. Thunder found a flat wooden tray and a cooking paddle that had been split from a cedar log; he also looked for gathering bags in which his special plants could be stored. The fish drying racks were easier to replace than move.

Sky offered to return with the villagers if Thunder and Slow Bear could manage the canoe alone. He and Carry could move all of Slow Bear's robes and bags for his new lodge. The decision had been made that storing the canoe near their village would prevent others from claiming it. As it turned out, that decision produced another fun story to tell.

The sun was not quite overhead when they watched the burdened line of villagers make their way back up the hill. Thunder and Slow bear had claimed a couple of the last robes and a couple sharp blades, which were in the canoe with the catching basket. It was large enough to fit a man in, and woven of fresh vine maple limbs that had dried into a stiff basket. With two paddles they would make good time, if Thunder could remember the way. By early afternoon, they were approaching the river below the waterfall. "Will you show me how the basket works?" Thunder asked Slow Bear. It was a bit awkward for them to lift the large basket without tipping the canoe. The leather straps, which would be looped over the back end of the canoe, looked worn, but still useable; a stone weight would function to keep the basket deep under water. It was just that easy to lower the strange contraption.

"Now paddle fast," Slow Bear said excitedly, "fish get in basket, and cannot get out."

Thunder smiled because Slow Bear was using a mixture of Salish and Kwakiutl. In just the short time they had been together, he was showing remarkable change. Slow Bear was not that slow at all.

They made one pass across the river near the falls before Thunder pulled the basket up to examine it. Nothing was in it, and he began to have doubts about the practicality of the effort. But he lowered again to give it another chance. They paddled rapidly away from the falls and then made a turn back toward it. When Thunder pulled the basket back up, he saw the flash of a silver fish. Now motivated, he lifted the basket quickly to find not one, but two medium sized red fish (Sockeye Salmon), more than he had ever caught in an afternoon. Slow Bear was laughing and clapping his hands. "We catch, now we eat!" he said happily. The basket was carefully lifted back into the canoe, and the fish dispatched with the stone weight. They hurried toward the shore, where they carried the canoe above the falls, and hid it upside down well off the trail, along with the basket. While Slow Bear carried the two robes, Thunder carried his gathering bag filled with bags, and the two fish, proudly presented on a stick through their gills. They would make quite a stir in the village when the folks saw that the red fish were returning.

Sky saw them making their up way toward the hill, several folks in their wake exclaiming at the good fortune. As he joined them Thunder suggested, "Tell Spear that if they want to join us, they will have the freshest red fish ever." Sky immediately turned to deliver the message that included a young lady he couldn't be near enough.

Once again the village was in the afternoon shadows of the trees, while Thunder's lodge was still in bright sunlight. The cooking rocks had been heating while the red fish were cleaned and cut into halves. Thunder recalled that the Sechelt cooks had advised him to give the fish heads and innards to the ground where the new seeds would be planted. "Feed the ground and it will fill you too," they had said. All that refuse was placed in a small cooking pouch and placed behind the lodge. They could take care of it in the morning.

He watched his family start up the gentle slope. On the cooking rocks he placed a large handful of fresh Bright leaves, then bones down, he heaped on the fish halves. They more than covered the cooking rocks. As the others arrived, full of happy stories of the items that had been salvaged, they marveled at Thunder's food preparation. Spear said to Sky, "No wonder you like to live here. If I could eat like this all ..." Basket bumped into him playfully.

"Slow Bear's basket works very well," Thunder said in greeting. "If it can catch fish now, think how easy it will be within the moon, when they are thick." There were other happy greeting words. Thunder noticed how flushed and happy Carry seemed.

It was time to turn the fish over. Thunder was hoping this would work as well as it did in his imagination. He placed the wooden tray beside the fish and carefully inserted the cooking paddle under one at a time, turning them skin-side down. Some of the Bright leaves clung to the cooked meat, adding to the flavor. While the second side cooked, they talked about the placement of Sky's new lodge, and Slow Bear's. When Thunder was convinced the red fish had cooked through he used the paddle once again to carefully lift the pink chunks onto the tray. He paused at the entrance to his lodge saying, "I come to you lodge, free of anger or fear. I embrace the peace and shelter you offer." He then invited them inside, delighted that they followed his example, even Slow Bear. They sat in a circle on the robes, feasting on the hot morsels. Sky gave Thunder an unspoken praise by nudging him. All in all, a fisherman could not ask for a better day.

"Slow Bear, did you move the cooking pouch with fish heads in it?" Thunder couldn't imagine why he would have. Morning had brought the reminder of an undone task.

"I don't know about it." Slow Bear answered, halfway afraid he had done a bad thing.

But when Thunder paid closer attention, he found disturbing tracks in the fresh dirt. One hind foot and two front feet Bear tracks! The culprit had stolen the pouch for a free snack, right beside Thunder's lodge! Spear and two others came up to verify the obvious; there was a marauding bear in the neighborhood.

It took three days to establish Sky's lodge at the lower entrance to the village. Some stubborn bushes had to be removed and a tiny bit of leveling of the site. It was a quiet place, tucked against the trees for shelter and shade. Slow Bear's only took two days, for it was smaller and at the base of the hill nearest Thunder's and adjacent to the large field that would become his growing domain. The young man seemed to be growing in stature and confidence with his new status. Perhaps losing his entire village, and living almost a year in isolation had been detrimental to his growth.

Then everyone awaited the red fish run, when the streams would be choked by the abundance. Sky decided that one important job left to do was to burn the weeds off the future garden site. It was done carefully to keep the fire inside the desired space.

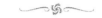

The Red Fish

Thunder said he would show Sky how the basket worked; then Sky could show Spear and the other men who were anxious to be successful fishermen. It took no time at all before they had four beautiful fish in the canoe, dispatched by a short club. Then four more joined them, and finally five more. The women who were going to clean and dry these fish would be hard pressed to keep up.

Spear insisted that he understood the procedure and wanted to be in the back of the canoe, pulling up the basket. It took them just four lifts of the basket to bring in fourteen more red fish. Slow Bear watched from the shore delighted by their catch. By evening the new drying rack was filled with over a hundred halves. A second rack was constructed and filled the next day. Thunder and Slow Bear were hurrying to dig small planting holes, which would receive the fish heads and innards now, and food seeds next spring. On the first day they managed to make sixty holes! But they needed three times that to complete one row, and by Thunder's calculations, they needed eleven more rows! They needed help. Sky came to help, then Carry, and finally Basket and Spring made it a workable process. Holes and fish parts soon filled the field.

The women's screams alerted the village to trouble. Instantly men were running to their assistance. They found a large black bear standing a short distance from the drying racks, bristled and growling menacingly. The women had thrown rocks and sticks, and made such noise that the hungry bear was momentarily held off. But hunger has a way of overcoming fear.

The bear charged the drying rack, which collapsed under the weight of fish plus the huge impact. Immediately the large mouth snapped up two fish halves. It was in the process of devouring his catch when the first arrow hit, high on the humped back, then a second hit lower and the bear screamed in anger. A spear, perhaps with a blade less sharp or perhaps because it hit a rib, sliced into the side of the furious animal, but did not penetrate with its lethal power. The bear whirled, roaring in pain, and disappeared into the thick brush. For several moments they could hear thrashing and growling in pain, then silence. "Perhaps it has died," one hunter offered. Another whispered, "It is waiting for us on more favorable ground for his attack." "It is bleeding, let it become weaker," a third offered. Another said simply, "I think it's gone." After much discussion with no conclusion, they finally returned to their lodges, but left armed guards to watch over the fish racks.

For those who captured the red fish, it had never been an easier season. The canoe and capturing basket had made it pleasure instead of labor. For those cleaning the fish, however, it was a frantic time. They probably cleaned about the same number of fish, but in far less time; they seemed behind the whole time. Happily the fifth rack was filled for the second time. There was adequate food for the entire winter.

Thunder remembered that it was time to look for the Bug Berry Trees (Elderberry). He knew what to look for and where. It was a matter of organizing the women and children to do the work of gathering the berries and leaves, then crushing them. The pulp should be scattered wherever they wanted no fleas. When he said it that way, the women organized and accomplished the task in an afternoon. Thunder wanted to gloat in his wisdom, but decided to wait to see the results. Perhaps if the fleas did not return, then he could gloat. He advised them that the final step in removing the fleas was the casting of fine ash from the cooking fires onto the Bug Berries. The children had such fun in that, the women had to run for shelter. The tiny faces were dusted and caked grey, which made Slow Bear remember a wonderful story his grandfather had told. He suggested to Thunder that on the next rainy afternoon, he would tell it to the children in the Long House.

The Storyteller

They didn't need to wait long for the rainy afternoon to come along. Thunder prepared a warm fire in the lodge, and while Slow Bear was preparing to tell the story, Sky and Carry walked through the village inviting the children. A cozy cluster gathered to hear the first of many teaching stories. Thunder hushed the children as Slow Bear backed into the dim room. When he turned around to speak there was a murmur of laughter and surprise for his face was caked with grey ash. Charcoal circles were from his cheeks to his forehead and a vertical line made the impression of a great beak, like a large owl.

"There was a family of owls who lived in the deep forest." Slow Bear's voice was lower in pitch and softer. "This family had four children: 'Ktlink' a son, 'Chuutl' a lovely daughter, and the little twin boys 'Sendel' and 'Tuldel.'" In a confiding voice, he said, "The Owl, as everyone knows is a silent hunter, flying on the softest wings through the night." The listeners were enthralled at the effectiveness of the storyteller.

"One night it came to pass that the boys wanted to go hunting after their father had placed them under their sleeping robes. Very quietly they waited for their father to go on his hunt." Slow Bear spread his arms like wings and circled the listeners, his head moving from side to side as though searching for a meal.

"One by one, the boys sneaked to the lip of the lodge, and" he hesitated dramatically, "flew into the night. They were not very good hunters, and were only having fun in the darkness. They flew through the forest without a sound." Again Slow Bear circled the children, looking one way and then another. "While they were far away, their father had caught a tasty mouse for them to eat. He flew directly to his lodge and landed on a limb. He called, 'Ktlink, my son, are you awake?' From the darkness Chuutl his daughter answered in her boyish voice, 'Yes father I am here,' whereupon the Father Owl gave the mouse to his son to eat. He then flew away to hunt for more." Slow Bear spread his arms and flew toward the entrance of the lodge and then returned.

"It wasn't very long before he found another juicy mouse and brought it back to his lodge, landing on the limb. 'Sendel, my son, are you awake?' Speaking in a confidential whisper Slow Bear said, "Now Chuutl had eaten as fast as she could to finish the first mouse. With a strained voice she answered, 'Yes father I am here,' whereupon the Father Owl gave the mouse to his son to eat, and he flew away to hunt for more." Once again Slow Bear spread his wings and encircled the listening children.

"Now the boy owls had flown to the far edge of the forest and decided that they should be on their way home for they were becoming very hungry." He had gone to the back corner of the lodge and was now returning to the circle. "Father Owl found the juiciest mouse of all and captured it for his family. When he landed on the limb he called, 'Tuldel, my son, are you awake?' Chuutl, who still had a mouse tail hanging from her mouth nearly choked as she said, 'Yes father I am here,' whereupon the Father Owl gave the mouse to his son to eat. He then flew away to hunt for more." Once again Slow Bear flew slowly to the front of the lodge and then circled back.

The boys were only halfway home when the father captured still another mouse, perhaps the largest of all. He brought it back to his lodge, landing on the limb and asking, 'Chuutl, my daughter, are you awake.' She was still chewing the last mouse and tried to answer, but it was only a mumble, 'Yes father, I'm here.'" Giggles of laughter demonstrated the children's delight in the story. "Whereupon Father Owl gave the mouse to his daughter to eat, then flew away to hunt for more."

"Chuutl had just swallowed the last morsel of mouse when the boys returned from their escapade. 'I'm hungry' said Ktlink. 'I'm hungry too,' said Sendel. 'My tummy hurts it is so empty', said Tuldel.' 'Be quiet you three, or you will get us in trouble for fooling Father Owl,' said Chuutl, stuffed so full of mouse that she thought she might burst."

"In the morning four little owls were nearly sick with tummy aches. Their faces were sad because of what they had done. But Father Owl smiled wisely, for of course, he had known the sound of his children's voices all along. Perhaps," Slow Bear emphasized the moral of the story, "they had learned a painful lesson in dishonesty, and the importance of always being truthful. 'HuHoo, Huhoo!'" Slow Bear spread his wings and glided out the entrance of the lodge to the delight of his enraptured listeners, who wanted more!

Sky said to Carry, "His voice was deeper, and more mellow."

"Yes," the delighted young lady answered, "he sounded like a New Bear instead of a Slow Bear." The topic of conversation throughout the village for the rest of the day was the gifted new Storyteller. They hoped it would rain again soon.

Four days later a shower began, so the villagers asked, "Will there be a story today?"

When Slow Bear was prepared, Sky once again went from lodge to lodge announcing the opportunity for the children to hear another tale from the woods. Fortunately the Long House could hold a larger crowd. Thunder suggested they be very quiet so Slow Bear could begin.

From the back of the lodge a voice said, "Deep in the forest there were neighbors who knew of one another, but didn't like the other. One of them was a coyote, who had long legs and was very fast, but was not very smart." Turning so the children could now see him, Slow Bear was wearing a mask over his nose and eyes made of a deer hide scrap. It was tied behind his head and had pointed ears that stood up. "The other was a fox, who was not as fast, but was very sneaky."

"Now it happened one day that the fast coyote caught a fat brown duck, and proudly brought it to his lodge, planning a fine supper. The fox saw it and immediately thought of a way it could be his instead. He complimented the coyote for such a fine catch, praising the speed and skill of his neighbor. He then offered to cook the duck for the coyote if he could just have the scraps." Slow Bear shook his head in warning.

"The coyote was pleased to have someone else do the work of cleaning and cooking the chubby bird, so he agreed, handing the duck to the fox." Now the storyteller made a worried face.

"The fox took the duck to his lodge where he exchanged it for a strip of dried seal he had stolen from a lodge of a person. This he took to the coyote, saying that he had overcooked the duck, and it was a little tough and dry, but with excellent flavor. As the coyote ate the meat he made a horrible face, for this was not the supper he had hoped to have." Slow Bear's face was twisted in comic dislike. "Later in his lodge, the fox relished every bite of juicy duck."

"Now it happened the next day that the fast coyote caught a fat brown bunny, and proudly brought it to his lodge, planning a fine supper. The fox saw it and devised a way it could be his instead. He complimented the coyote for such a fine catch and told him he had an extra collection bag to carry it to his lodge. He actually had two bags in his hands, one empty, and one with grass and a piece of wood. When the coyote said he would welcome a collecting bag, the fox put the bunny in the empty bag, but gave the grass and wood to the coyote." The story teller's voice was a whisper filled with conspiracy. "When he got to his lodge and reached in the bag, the coyote was very angry. He went back to the Fox to get his meal but was met by an excited face.

"Did you feel the earthquake?" the fox said in a panic. It was Taghil the forest shadow spirit that shakes the earth to remind people how small they really are! He changes food into grass and wood. Oh my!" The fox seemed very perplexed and the coyote believed him for a bit, so he went back to his hungry lodge, while the prankster fox was enjoying another big meal."

"The coyote was so angry that for three days he dug a great deep hole on the trail. At first he thought he might catch another bunny, but then it occurred to him that the fox would try to get it, so he dug a trap for the fox. When it was deep enough, he called out in a loud voice, 'Hiee! I've caught a big fat rabbit! Hiee!" Slow Bear was dancing with joy.

"Of course the fox heard, and of course the fox ran to see what he might get from the coyote. Blump! He fell in the trap! He tried to jump out, but it was too deep. He tried to climb, but the sides were too steep. "Help me, coyote! Help me neighbor!"

"The coyote said, 'Oh did you fall into Taghil's trap? I would help you but I must see if I can catch a duck or a bunny for supper." As the coyote hurried away, a great bear came strolling along the trail, and found himself … a wonderful … supper."

Slow Bear removed the fox mask from his face, and sharing in a quiet voice said, "If you play many tricks on your neighbor, you will end up in a trap." He slowly walked out of the Long House. The story was over, but the listener's appetite for more was growing. Thunder realized that this talented man had been grossly underestimated by whoever had first called him Slow Bear. He was bright and very essential to the village future.

One gloomy afternoon, Slow Bear invited the children to the Long House for another story. When they arrived, they found no fire to light their space, so they sat quietly in the darkness. When the flaps at the front were closed it was very dark inside, then Slow Bear began.

"There was a time when Raven had only darkness to fly in; he flapped and flew without knowing where he was going or where he had been. He thought to himself, 'I should have a way to see, so I don't get lost.' He thought on it for several days. He thought about stars in the sky, and a moon and a bright sun, until they were just as we see them. 'Grawk!' said the Raven, which means 'Thank you.'" Slow Bear opened the lodge flap, enabling his listeners to see a bit.

"The Raven was very tired of flying for he had no place to land, so he thought to himself, 'If I had someplace to land, I could rest.' He thought on it for several days, until there appeared a piece of dirt he could land on." Pretending to try to hold his balance, the storyteller said, "But it wasn't very big, so he thought about it much more. He thought about hills and valleys and mountains and trees, lakes and streams until they were just as we see them. 'Grawk!' said the Raven, which means 'Thank you.'"

"The Raven was lonely all by himself, so he thought it would be nice to share all this with other creatures, then he could talk with them. He thought on it for many days; he thought of animals small and large, birds that sing and others that swim. He thought on it until there appeared all the wonderful animals we see today. 'Grawk!' said the Raven, which means 'Thank you.'"

"Then the Raven thought to himself, 'Who will look after all this while I'm flying far away? There should be someone who cares for the forests and lakes, the shores and the trails.' One day while he was dining on clams, he thought about a human being. He thought for several days until there appeared a man and a woman just as we see them. But the Raven was silent, for he was not sure that they would care for the land as he intended, if they would kill only what they can eat, and are mindful of the woods and water. Today when you hear the voice of the Raven speak, look around and see if there is someone protecting the Raven's work. 'Grawk!' says the Raven in gratitude. 'Grawk!' which means 'thank you.'"

As Thunder stepped to the open flap, he said, "Today we have learned to speak Raven. We can say to Slow Bear, 'Grawk!' Thank you!" As the children poured out, some even flapped their arms like wings, shouting, "Grawk! Thank you, Slow Bear!" The Long House was becoming a place of lessons, and none could be happier than Thunder, or Slow Bear the Teacher.

―✥―

A Tragic Conclusion

―✥―

The leaves of the forest had turned from green to brilliant yellow to dull brown, and then they fell to the forest floor, making it look lifeless and empty. Rains were frequent, but this morning there had been a heavy coat of frost. Everyone in the village was grateful for their warm sleeping robes, and anxious to remain within them, until they heard the scream of a man's voice in the distance. There were muffled words, and another scream. Many were now running toward the sound of trouble. They scattered in search of it. Spear was carrying his hunting spear, and thought it might have been wiser to bring the hunting bow. Directly in front of him he heard another desperate cry.

He was on the scene before he expected. The form of a man lay under the pawing claws of a bear. Without thinking if there might be others nearby to help, he launched his attack at the vulnerable side of the animal. His spear point drove deeply into the black fur, and now the bear screamed, and spun on its attacker. The violent motion ripped the shaft of the spear from his hands and for a heartbeat, Spear knew that this was a contest he could not win. Bright pink froth oozed from the spear wound. The animal was injured in the lung, but it would have more than enough time to finish this battle. The bear rose up on his back legs, head hanging down in the moment before lunging.

Spear felt a body dart in front of his, as a bow launched an arrow into the exposed throat of the bear. The momentum of the archer carried them both away from the bear's range. Spurting blood from the wound was proof that now the bear's battle time was limited to one more breath; as it crashed in a heap, they knew it didn't even have that. Sticking out from its shoulder were two remnants of arrow shafts, and a spear wound. This angry wounded animal had been near them since the first fish rack.

A trembling Sky looked at Spear and said, "That was very close. Are you injured?"

Spear shook his head as he made his way toward the still body lying behind the bear. Others arrived at the scene ready to help, Thunder among them.

The man's body was gaunt, naked and dirty, his hair a tangled mat. The bear had bitten him repeatedly, and claw marks on the side of his head suggested that the bear had slapped him viciously. His head was angled oddly, suggesting that he had suffered no longer than that blow. When Spear turned the body over, he gasped. The ragged facial scar confirmed his worst fear. It was his son Camas.

"Oh no!" Thunder cried out, "No, No! He is my brother. I did this to him!" He wept uncontrollably. "The lodge was not worth his life!" he sobbed. "I didn't mean to damage his handsome face!" The village men were uneasy, seeing the depth of their Shaman's grief. "I pleaded for him!" Thunder finally said quietly. No words could fill the emptiness they all shared.

Spear placed his hand on Thunder's bent back, saying, "I could not choose his path, nor could you. He lost his own way." Someone brought a robe which they could use to carry his body.

The villagers helped carry the body up the hill to the sacred ground. A scraped place had been prepared near Hawk's grave. There was much weeping when the rocks were placed on top of the mound of dirt. It was still and cold.

As they walked back toward the village, Spear said to Sky, "In an instant that bear would have been on me. Thank you for quick thinking, and a perfect arrow." Sky accepted the gratitude with a slow nod.

Several silent steps later, Sky said, "This may not be a good time to bring this up; on the other hand, it might be the perfect time. I would be honored to share a steaming pouch with you, if you feel like stopping at my lodge sometime soon. I know how Thunder makes it. I'd like to ask you something important."

Walking two strides behind them, Carry caught her breath.

An Abundant Beginning

The fall hunt went well; more deer than usual, and there was adequate sunshine to dry strips. With deer strips and all the salmon the village had stored, there would be enough food to get through the winter, regardless of how terribly long it might be. Before the rains set in, Sky took Carry into his lodge, and Thunder walked with the wind back to the Sechelt village to talk again with the seed planters. He wanted to be sure about the precise time to place the seeds in the ground.

On a sunny day after a storm, Thunder convinced Sky that they could cross the big water in the canoe. To their surprise the journey took less than half a day. Sky visited Knapper's lodge, happy to see his father and mother again. He was eager to share with his family the pleasant stories of the Kwakiutl village, and invite them to visit. While he was enjoying the return to his village, Thunder went on to the Haida village where he shared seeds of the Three Sisters with Klaw and Helps. His heart was happy to see them again. They were surprised to see the development of a true Shaman in this young man whom they held in great respect. Thunder could have remained there longer, but knew that the weather would soon be too stormy to cross the big water until spring. There was a young woman named Breath, who seemed extraordinarily winsome to Thunder. They spoke one afternoon, her happy eyes, and sweet voice were impossible for him to overlook, or forget. She listened with a playful smile as he told her of the friendship he had found with Sky, the crooked nose Salish. She wanted to know more about his family and his village. He promised to continue the conversation when he returned in the spring. He did sincerely invite them all to visit the Kwakiutl village.

The winter was a slow time for the Kwakiutls. Their greatest challenge was keeping enough dry wood for their lodge fires. There were two brief snowfalls, and a lot of rain. It was a time that Thunder could teach the children words from the Salish and Haida. By springtime, Slow Bear could tell them stories in either language.

After the fourth full moon of the fresh year, as the sun was filling more of each day, the seeds were planted where the salmon heads had been buried. This time there was no shortage of volunteers who had a keen interest in the results of this effort. Thunder explained the process as he had been told. With a boring spike, a hole was made as deep as the span of a man's hand, and two seeds deposited. He watched as the work was accomplished, knowing the satisfaction of teaching a fresh development.

Slow Bear spent most days with the new sprouts, now covering the field, and the many children he had recruited to keep the food patch free of rodents that might try to feed there. He also had a special totem that he carved all winter long. When he was finally finished, it took most of the strong men in the village to erect the Thunderbird above the Long House. On the following rainy afternoon, Slow Bear told the children this story, accompanied by Sky playing a happy rhythm on the new singing drum, "Thump, bump, bump, bump; Thump, bump, bump, bump."

"No one has ever seen a Thunderbird," Slow Bear said in a quiet voice as the drum continued, "but we have all heard one. The Thunderbird is a spirit creature that feeds on clouds. His great beak rips through the clouds." His hands clapped together with his arms stretched out in front of him. "It makes fire, and an extremely loud rumble." As the story-teller said the word, he clapped again, and let the sound reverberate on the singing drum as thunder is apt to do.

"A village once needed a spirit bird because it had been attacked by an illness that threatened to overcome everyone who lived there. They were so weak they couldn't help themselves, and had little hope. Many were near death. High in the clouds," Slow Bear spread his arms like giant wings and circled the listeners in a rhythmic dance with the singing drum, "the Thunderbird saw their troubles and swooped down to them. No one saw it coming, but within a short time, they knew it was blessing them. They felt stronger, and then they began to walk around." He continued to dance around the listeners faster and faster, "The sickness was letting go of them. Soon they were well and gave the spirit bird happy thanks. It blessed them with abundant fish, and even more deer. The new growing field promised food for every lodge. The village found a Shaman, and a story-teller who loves the children. Did the Thunderbird do all of that for them?" The children nodded their heads, but were not completely convinced.

"Now, when the rumble of thunder comes down the mountain, the village people turn and raise their hands. They thank the Thunderbird for making their story so happy; their village is a place where all the people want to live in peace. So, when you hear it, you do not need to run and hide in fear. The Thunderbird is seeking to bless you too. It will fill you with courage and strength. Just turn toward the sound and raise your hand; say, 'thank you, Thunderbird, for making me strong!' Can you do that?" Now all the heads nodded, and every hand was raised. "Thank you, Thunderbird, for making me strong!" Their voices repeated the chant to the beat of the drum. Slow Bear was teaching them pride in their history, and love for their village, as well as courage in a noisy storm.

The warm summer sun ripened the beans first. The children had been given the task of patrolling the field to frighten away the Crows and squirrels that would have happily fed first. When the pods were harvested, Slow Bear was given the task of dividing a portion to each lodge, reserving enough seeds to plant next year's crop. Some of the pods were eaten raw. They were such a novel new discovery. Most of the pods, however, were opened and the beans placed on a robe in the sun. When they were dried, storage bags promised to provide a new food for the winter,

The corn crop was next, and it exceeded even the optimistic hopes of Thunder. Once again the division for each lodge was surprising, even after Slow Bear set aside enough to plant next year. Again the drying process gave them enough to be ground and made into corn cakes. There was happy laughter that worries of hunger were a thing of the past.

Spring, Thunder's youngest sister, discovered a way to weave the long corn leaves into a mat that she placed under Spear's sleeping robe. It was not only more comfortable than sleeping on the hard ground, it was also a pleasant fragrance in the lodge. Soon other women were weaving mats for their floors.

The Squash were ready to harvest when the leaves began to turn golden. Not even Thunder was prepared for the size of this food. Each lodge was given at least three great round fruit. Thunder shared the instructions he had received. "Use a chopping blade to open it. The seeds are of first interest. Bring half of them back to Slow Bear for next year. Separate the seeds from the slippery interior, which is edible if you want to try to roast it. Dry the seeds first on a robe; they can be saved, or roasted and eaten like nuts when the shell is cracked. The heavy flesh of the Squash should be cut into small squares about the size of your knuckle." He bent his finger, demonstrating the size. These squares will dry just as the other food has. You must make sure it is dried all the way through or it will rot during the winter, which would be a sad loss." He smiled broadly as he completed the instructions. "Believe me, I have tasted the Three Sisters, and they are wonderful." Laughter filled the village that had a Long House, a great storyteller, a garden, a wonderful new location, no fleas, and most of all, a Shaman that worked to make them healthy,

"Thank you, Thunderbird, for making me strong!" indeed.

Finis: Book Two, Feast in the Dirt

Book 3

Unexpected Wealth

Table of Contents

The Rat

Kahota awoke slowly, like one swimming through a cold dense fog. It had been an increasingly difficult two years, as he had coped on his own. The sadness began when the Inuit men went seal hunting out on the ice, and took the women with them. That was very unusual, especially when they didn't return. He stayed with his grandparents until the food ran out. His grandfather died first. Four year old Kahota helped pull the naked cold body out onto the ice. He didn't understand why they just left him there. But a child learns to live with those large questions, believing that if the answers will come, they will come later in time.

After eating the last dog, the two of them huddled under the hide covers trying to stay warm, until his grandmother stopped breathing. There was no one else to help, so he struggled to drag her frail cold body out onto the ice, weeping from grief and fear. The silence of the frozen winter terrified him, so he did the only thing he could do. He crawled under the covers and waited to die, dreaming of laughing adults, and happier days. The delirium caused him to hear voices calling for his attention. He sang with them and laughed. Then he wept again, for these voices were real.

The hunting party almost missed the old Inuit igloos; they were like drifts in the snow. One of the men suggested looking in to see if there might be anything to scavenge. That's how they found an emaciated and semiconscious Kahota. They took the robes and meager possessions they could use and placed them on top of him in their sled. They also gave him some fresh blubber to eat, and promised that they would take him to his grandparents. The four year old child was at the whim of charity's compassion.

Over the next four years that sad drama was repeated several times. He was not old enough to be helpful, just another mouth to feed. His migration was steadily southward, perhaps because there was less ice in that direction, and more people to pass him along to. There was no one who cared enough to offer true nurture to the child. Not surprisingly, Kahota learned lessons of survival, deceit and dishonesty. They called him "the Rat," because of his unkept appearance and behavior. He frequently foraged at night for scraps of food.

Finally, one fateful day, he was caught stealing a small stone knife by a woman cracking marrow out of a moose bone. In her irritation, she hit him with the bone, intending only to discipline him. A needle-sharp splinter on the end of the bone, however, pierced the side of his face, entering the soft tissue of his eyelid and passing into the delicate organ beneath it. Kahota howled like a wounded animal, for he was. Quickly the woman attempted to correct the damage by removing the long sliver of bone, but the irreversible damage had been done. When the bleeding eventually stopped, there was drainage which continued until the pain ended.

His eye atrophied into a dark husk in an empty socket. The woman's constant weeping in remorse became more than the man could tolerate. He asked a seal hunting Haida group to take the Rat with them. So once again Kahota was a problem relocated. This time, however, there was no family that would offer him shelter. He was placed in the end of a large wooden boat near the carcasses of their kill. The journey was terribly long across in immense body of water. He was terrified for several reasons.

Long after Kahota had given up hope, they arrived at a place that would one day be called Port Hardy. The men, speaking in a language that he could not understand, pulled him out of the boat and threw his robe and empty bag at his feet. They told him, by angry gestures, to be on his way; to leave. They spoke as he had heard others shout at an unwanted dog.

So began the days of begging. He was so hungry he stopped at the first lodge he could find. He asked if they would share some of their food, in Inuit of course. The man shouted angrily and waved him away. There was even a motion to throw something at him. Desperation urged Kahota to try again, and then again, until a gentle woman offered him a strip of dried seal. It was little in her eyes, but tremendous in his. It meant he would survive.

As the days passed he tried, without knowing their language, to indicate that he was injured. He found a walking stick, and discovered that if he turned his face so they would see only his empty eye socket, there was a greater chance they would be generous. He was diminutive for an eight year old. One sweet woman was so touched by his condition that she gave him an old gathering bag with three strips of dried seal. He would have enough food for the next day.

He was nearing the end of the village, for he could see the forest pressing in. There could be one more attempt to put food in his bag. He called into the lodge that he was a lost child who was so hungry, about to parish. To his amazement a voice in Inuit spoke back that there was plenty to eat inside. "Please come in by the fire." Kahota's heart soared. He would be warm again!

The old man who greeted the sad youngster, spoke in Inuit, telling him a long story as he shared a strip of seal. He had been a happy husband and father until his wife died. Then his daughters went to live in other men's lodges and his sons had gone south down the coast to live in a hunting village. They brought him deer and red fish. There were always clams to dig, but he was very lonely, and glad to meet Kahota.

The lad explained that his family had died about four years ago, when he was only four years old. He had been passed from lodge to lodge by the Intuits, until the problem with the angry lady who had pierced his eye. Now he was getting by the only way he could, by begging.

"You can stay here with me," the old man said warmly. "There is enough food, and I can teach you to speak Haida. That's what these people speak." They had enjoyed a couple strips of dried deer and a delicacy the old man had called "corn cakes." Kahota was very satisfied with the prospects.

Through the evening the wrinkled teacher had given him the words of greeting, and the phrase, "Please help me. I have no food." He had instructed the eager learner to be gracious and speak a word of gratitude. "It is not necessary to tell them you are Inuit. They will already know that by your speech, and smell." He chuckled at his own humor. The fire had nearly burned itself out. "You are welcome to spread your robe on this side of the fire for the night."

It had been quite a while since Kahota had been so comfortable. He was warm and well fed; the only thing that could have made it better is if he had a bath. Under his robes he was almost asleep when the old man, now naked, crawled under the robe with him. His hands sought to touch the lad in unwelcome ways and his intent was clear. He intended to mount him like a woman!

"Ieee," Kahota screamed. "Ieee, you are the evil trickster! Ieee!" He leaped up, grabbing his robe and bag, he ran out the front of the lodge. "Ieee! Evil trickster!" There was, however, a smile on his face because he had grabbed another robe along with his, and another gathering bag with strips of deer, and a couple sharp blades in it. "Ieee," he continued to shout as he ran into the dark. Finally, in the forest under a Cedar tree, whose boughs touched the ground, he made a comfortable site that would be dry. Warmed by two robes, and safe, he slept well.

The Rat begged his way from village to village, season by season for two years. The rainy and snowy days actually worked to his advantage for he looked so miserable, which he was most of the time anyway. It was difficult for anyone to deny him assistance. One summer morning he tried to steal a canoe and received a severe beating that required many days of recuperation, which again he worked to his advantage. He was a pathetic creature. While other ten year old boys had learned the language, history, and customs of their village, how to fish and hunt, Rat had focused on the chore of surviving.

A Chance Meeting

One autumn morning Kahota awoke slowly, like one swimming through a cold dense fog. He ached from prolonged demand on his frail body with minimal food. He would weep if it could change his situation. It had been six days since his last village, and three days since his last meal. He pulled his robe closer around him, and struggled to find the trail he had found yesterday. Where there was a trail, there would be a village to find food. He pressed through the brush, hoping he was going in the right direction. The sun was sliding down toward evening when he smelled a cooking fire. He had found the trail, but no village.

Sunset was giving way to twilight when he finally came upon the camp of two travelers. There were no weapons so they were not hunters. Rat's hope was kindled. He stood at the edge of the firelight, waiting for their invitation, or rejection. The taller of the two noticed him and beckoned him to join them, but he was speaking a different language. In Haida, Rat asked for their assistance. He was very hungry, and lost.

In Haida they asked the location of his village, but he didn't understand. They asked again in Salish. Rat said again in Haida that he was very hungry, and lost. He took hesitant steps toward the fire. The tall man and the other studied Rat as he approached. He was filthy, hunched under a heavily worn robe, and they noticed the hollow eye socket. The tall one asked in Inuit, "Where is your village?"

"I came from the land of the ice," the Inuit words tumbled out. "My family died. Hunters took me to another village. I have no home and no food. Can you help me?" His eye caught the beautiful walking stick that was stuck in the ground by the robes spread for the night. It was adorned with a stone, feathers and a bird crafted from bone. The wood seemed oiled and smooth. He could trade much food for such a treasure. He was not aware that this particular walking stick was already famous in the region, and would be instantly identified as stolen.

"What is your name," the tall man asked, as the other one beckoned the scruffy beggar to come by the fire.

"My father gave me the name Kahota, but I am called Rat, because I live off the scraps of others." He accepted the deer strip that was offered. Quickly he ate it. Then he received a corn cake, and again he ate without acknowledging his gratitude, but he did take a small side-step toward the walking stick. He was offered another deer strip. He took another side-step as he reached for the dried meat. In an instant he leaped to the walking stick, pulled it from the ground, and sprinted toward the edge of the forest now shrouded in darkness. They had no weapons, and he had a head-start. He was confident that he would succeed again at gaining an advantage. He could hear the frantic rustle of feet behind him but he was already halfway to the tree line. The sudden pain in his back was like nothing he had ever felt, a gigantic blow from an unseen assailant. He could not catch a breath, and his legs no longer obeyed the demand for speed. He crashed face down into the dirt.

The tall man retrieved the walking stick without concern for Rat's desperate struggle for air. He handed the stick to the other man who had a simple sling in his hand. The stone that Thunder had cast had found its target in the center of the back of the fleeing culprit. Because the Rat had a robe wrapped around him, no bones had broken, which surely would have occurred on a less protected gaunt body.

Sky returned to the gasping body, grasping a handful of matted hair. He pulled Rat to his feet, inviting any struggle which would have been met with immediate force. "You are a foul Rat, a rodent that should be smashed." He was speaking in Kwakiutl, which sounded like gibberish to Rat. "We offered you hospitality and you saw only opportunity for disrespect. Tomorrow we will offer you to the Salish as a slave." He was wrapping a hide strap around Rat's neck without concern for his comfort. Sky dragged him back to the campsite where he carefully bound him to a stout tree. Rat was placed in a kneeling position, his back against the tree, and his feet tied around the tree; his elbows were also tied securely behind the tree and his hands bound behind him. If he tried to free himself, the strap around his neck would tighten dangerously. Speaking once again in Inuit, Sky said, "We offered you food. You have turned it into an insult." He slapped the side of the unprotected head.

"I think he understands that we disapprove of his behavior." Thunder was watching Sky secure the prisoner. For just a moment he reflected that Sky himself had been bound in a similar manner by the Haida.

Sky growled in Inuit, "If he tries to run again, I will take out his other eye." The words sounded threatening, but the expression on his face, which the prisoner could not see, reflected a more reasonable man.

Thunder said quietly, "I didn't know you are so familiar with Inuit."

"There are two Inuit lodges in our village. I hoped it would come in handy someday. I'm thinking I will try to 'sell' this rodent to one of them." The blooming smile said that Sky was enjoying this conflict now that the outcome was determined. He looked up into the trees as a breath of wind rustled the leaves.

It may have been the longest night of Rat's life. It certainly was the most uncomfortable. In the kneeling position, if he tried to relieve the tension in his legs by bending his knees, the strap around his neck pinched tight to strangle him. He was securely tied. Finally, as the far mountains began to show an outline in the dawn, the shorter man slid out from under his robe; the other must have been awakened, for he rose also.

The first man, whom Rat was coming to understand was in charge, came over to him and offered a drinking pouch sip of water. Then carefully, he untied Rat's hands and feet. The band around his neck remained. Rat understood that he was not released, only freed enough to relieve himself, and wait for their directions.

The tall one, who seemed to have a half smile and a crooked nose, ordered him to sit. They ate small portions of dried red fish, and then offered Rat a small chunk of wood looking stuff, that he chose not to accept. With a shrug, the tall man popped it into his own mouth with some satisfaction, saying in Inuit, "You will learn in time that some things that are new to you are really very good." The dried squash was a new development from their village.

A New Village

After they had rolled their robes for travelling, they found Rat's where he had left it last night. There was a collection bag with three other bags inside; the only other contents were scraps of leather, a worn pair of moccasins, and six sharp blades and a couple broken ones. Sky suggested that they leave this stolen trash in the bushes. Speaking in Inuit, he wanted the prisoner to know the distain he was feeling.

Once on the familiar trail, Sky set the pace with Thunder guarding the prisoner, who felt the sharp prod of the walking stick only twice during the day. The second time the sharp point found the tender stone bruise, and he cried out in pain. The afternoon sun was still high in the sky when they entered the Salish village. Sky guided them directly to the lodge of Chief Otter, who would determine the future of the young thief. He agreed that the idea of "selling" the urchin to the Inuit lodge would be the very best solution.

The first try was futile; there were already five children to feed. While they agreed that this was a humane solution, they urged Sky to take the Rat to the other Inuit lodge. Before they went there, they removed the strap around his neck. Then they made their appeal on his behalf, setting aside any incrimination for the attempted theft. Thunder urged them to bath him immediately and treat him like a member of their family. He would be a year older than their daughter and three years older than their only son. Sky asked permission to visit Knapper's lodge; Thunder encouraged him to go, but said he would attend the clean-up of Kahota.

The following hour was transforming. He could not remember a real bath, so sitting in the shallow brook was exhilarating, even if the water was a bit chilly. Thunder helped scrub his back with Happy Leaf, and then tried to comb the tangles from his long hair. Finally dry, with his long hair tied carefully with a leather string, and dressed in fresh clothes that had mysteriously appeared, Kahota genuinely smiled for the first time in a long while. He felt human! There was a glimmer of hope for him.

By the time Sky returned, he could translate the negotiations for Thunder. Kahota was near tears repeatedly, as he accepted their conditions, and offer to live in their lodge as a son. He knew what it was like to have no care, and no hope. Now in one day his situation had reversed. Suddenly he remembered the Haida words of gratitude he had been taught two years ago. They poured out passionately, surprising both Sky and Thunder, and pleasing his new Inuit family. Before leaving them, Sky explained his decision to live with the Kwakiutl, and described the splendors of their new village.

They bid Kahota farewell with an honest embrace, and a blessing on the lodge. What an amazing change of events in just one day. The wind was miraculous, indeed.

When the moon was completely dark, they knew it was time to return to their lodges. Thunder had been considering the behavior of the water. He understood that the big water was most agitated when the moon was full, and when the wind showed its strength. When leaving their side of the big water it was most calm if they waited until the water was completely full. As it ran out on a calm day, they were aided by its flow. The same thing was true when they wanted to return to the Morning Mountain side. If they waited until the water was fully out on a windless day, they could cross in less than half a day. The barrier of distance had lost its challenge.

Some Good - Some Terrible

Before the winter set in with its cold grip, two major changes occurred for the Kwakiutl village. The first was the popularity of Slow Bear and the Long House stories became so popular they were made a daily occurrence. When the sun was above the mountain, the children would make their way up the hill. It was such a constant parade that a new path had to be made to protect the hillside. Now they went a bit further up the main trail before they turned toward the Long House, walking across the lip of the hill. Thunder smiled when he saw that their mothers had given them a small gathering bag with a corn or squash snack, intending the children to be with Slow Bear longer than one story. He expanded the listening time to include making image marks on the dirt floor. They were becoming artists as well as informed students.

His library of stories included: Taghil the trickster; Eagle the strong leader; Beaver; the pranks of coyote; the strong family (pack) ties of Wolf; Sad Skunk; Frog Lady; Salmon Boy; Dancing Moose; Lost Bear; Silly Seal; Orca the Mighty, and the Children Who

Misbehaved. No wonder the children wanted to be in attendance.

Sky realized that, with all these children, another waste pit would serve the Long House, and its many friends. He recruited a couple other men to help him place and dig out the pit a safe, yet discreet distance behind the lodge. The convenience was not lost on Thunder or the others who used it.

The second major change occurred with the appearance of Diego the Spaniard, a Trapper. With his woman, Star from the Makah tribe, he was looking for fox and beaver pelts. They approached Sky's lodge because it was the first one at the entrance to the village.

"Halloo!" the woman called. "Halloo, is anyone there?" Sky stepped out first, followed by a curious Carry. "Do you speak Salish," she asked.

"Yes," Sky replied, "and Haida, or Kwakiutl, which is this village. What do you want?'

"This is Diego, a Trapper," she introduced the man who was not dressed in hide clothes, but something like moss which was the same color. "We would like to speak with the hunters of your village." She was polite and soft spoken, even clearing her throat to be better understood. Sky was dubious none the less.

"What do you want with us?" Sky asked again, a bit more aggressively.

The woman smiled warmly, holding out her hands, saying, "We do not want to disturb you. We are searching for fox or beaver skins." She paused to cough raggedly. "We can trade for them."

Sky was wishing that Thunder could be here to answer the woman. He would know what the wind thought about this pair. "I'm sure no one in this village has any skins to trade. You are wasting our time here."

He turned and went back into his lodge. Carry watched as the man and woman traded a quick conversation.

The woman said more loudly, "We have a snare that will help you catch many fox and beaver. We will wait by the stream until the sun is high for those who are interested." As she coughed again, the man held up the pelt of a red fox, stroked it across his face, and smiled broadly. "It will take so little time to learn about this opportunity," she said finally. She had spoken loud enough for most of the nearby lodges to hear also. Briefly, that would spread to all the other lodges that hadn't heard.

In all, eight hunters wandered down the trail to the stream. There they heard the trapper's proposal, translated by the woman. She held up a braided line about twice as long as the span of a man's outstretched arms. It had a noose at the end and a small loop about a quarter above it. "Find a well used trail by the water's edge for a beaver, or near a fox's den," she instructed. "Bend over a stout limb with spring in it and attach the loose end of the snare." She had to pause, coughing again. "Find a small stub that will hold the limb down, and slide the little loop over it. Then hang the noose," she coughed once again, "over the trail where the animal will hook it over its head. As it struggles to get free, it will pull the loop off the stub, and the limb will spring up. Most of the time the animal is choked to death, but it may also just be hanging there waiting for your final touch." She cleared her voice. The man spoke to her in a language none of them recognized.

She made the offer they were waiting to hear. "We have a few of these snares left. If you would like to trade for one, three strips of deer or seal or four strips of red fish will be accepted." She cleared her voice, and concluded, "Next spring we will be back through this way, trading for the pelts you have gathered." She held up a shining red stone about the size of a nut. It was clear as water, but had reflections glittering like a star. Hanging on a fine leather strip, it made a necklace of superb quality. "Please give this to your chief as a sign of our intent to make your village more beautiful. If you would like one of these for your woman, just two pelts will trade for it. The hunters crowded in to look closer at the snare, and of course, at the necklace.

As the morning ended, they had each acquired at least one snare, and contact with a contagious infection that would develop into an outbreak that would challenge Thunder's healing abilities.

Sickness!

The coughing began seven days later, a hacking strangling sort of cough. All eight of the hunters who had purchased snares were afflicted. The puzzle to Thunder was that Chief Bear also fell ill. The vomiting and diarrhea began the next day and then followed the hot skin. All nine men fell gravely ill.

Sky pondered how the illness had gotten into the men. "Perhaps she rubbed them with it," he guessed.

"But the Chief was not there to be touched," Thunder countered.

"Perhaps it was in her shadow that fell on them," the tall friend rethought the cause.

"And perhaps," Thunder was digging deep into the matter, "it was a filth that was on the leather straps of the snares and necklace. That is the only thing they all touched."

At first Thunder had simply suggested to the women that they might put some Bright Leaf in a boiling bag for them to sip. But when they became delirious, Thunder suggested that they be moved to the Long House, where he could try to administer more medicinal care. With Sky's help, all nine were made as comfortable as possible.

Three of the men became semiconscious. When, after another two days, it became evident that none of them could drink the steaming cups, Thunder filled a boiling bag with Bleeder, Bright, and Juniper berries and mashed cones. He kept adding water as the steam filled the closed Long House. After two more days, when it seemed the nine were nearing death, Thunder began to place happy leaf and Cap flowers onto the burning coals in the center of the Long House, filling it with smoke. It was all he could imagine doing, but wait.

He and Sky began to experience the cough just as the hunters were showing signs of recovery. Thunder tried to remember the on-set of the illness. "It takes ten days for the sickness to poison us, and hopefully ten days to put it out of our bodies." Several of the women began to cough as well. "We must boil the snares and necklace to kill the shadow on it," he suggested. Eventually the illness made its way to every lodge, but with less intensity as time went by. The Long House was busy for three waves of the illness. The good news was that each wave was less severe than the first one. The bad news was that the Long House would have a lingering odor of sickness and cure for a long while. The news they would learn in the future was that their village was not the only one infected. But it was the only one where there were no fatalities. The efforts of Sky and Thunder had saved the village a second time. Little did they know that this exposure to outside infections had given them the start to an immunity that would protect their village in the future. Finally Slow Bear could invite the children back for storytelling.

One important result of the illness was realized at the council meeting. Both Sky and Thunder were invited to sit in. Chief Bear asked Thunder if the Smoking Pipe could be ready. He was recommending that the Elders include these two courageous young men. It was a happy time to remember, a time for prayers.

Another important result was an inventory of medicinal leaves and stems. Thunder looked at his nearly empty gathering bags. The battle with the illness had exhausted his cache. "What I should do," he shared with Slow Bear, "is bring some of each plant here, and keep them growing so we will never run out." The frosts of winter had killed most of the leaves, but the two determined men hunted and up-rooted several bags of plants that were relocated around the Long House. The Junipers were the most challenging, for they were woody plants, like trees. "Let's just see if we can get small starts," Thunder suggested. "They will grow, in time." Perhaps the most spectacular plantings were the Dry Flowers planted on the hillside in front of the Long House. They would spread until the entire hill was draped in yellow blossoms. Happy Leaf and Bright had their place in the back, and would prosper as well. Cap lined the path into the Long House, which in late summer would be a spectacular addition.

Winter

After such a challenging beginning, the winter passed with little drama. There were three births and no fatalities. Seven Fox fell victim to the new snares, and three Beavers joined them. The women sang happy songs.

On one of the quiet days of early spring, the village had Salish visitors. The hunting canoe from the other side of the big water brought Knapper, the Inuit named Chuiku, and two other hunters, along with the six explorers who remembered the way. The Inuit said he had thought long on Sky's description of this village, and he wanted to see it for himself. The visit gave the Kwakiutl village an opportunity to share their bountiful harvest, and build a reputation for generosity, as they offered the Long House for the visitor's comfort. Knapper delivered a gift to Thunder from a charming young woman from the Haida village named Breath. She had crafted a hood from rabbit skins, fur side in, to give him protection from the rain and cold. Before they returned to their own lodges, there were requests from four of the visitors who sought permission to relocate to this Kwakiutl village.

Slow Bear approached Thunder, one bright morning, with a question. "Do you think we grew enough food last year, or should I try to make three more rows?" Before he answered, Thunder was aware how much change had blossomed in this young man, who had at first been thought to be slow, and now was evidently one of the village's more thoughtful men.

"How could we add room in our garden?" Thunder answered, seeking more information.

"If I could recruit a couple of the older boys to clear the brush from each side, we could add a row of Squash, and by moving the beans, we could add two more rows of corn." The suggestion was delivered with a confident smile that suggested he had given this considerable thought.

"Slow Bear, you are our Chief Grower indeed! That's a very good idea; we may have four new lodges soon." Before it was time to put the new seeds in the ground, the expanded space had been cleared. Their village was growing, along with their appreciation for a young man whom they had invited into their hearts only as an act of compassion.

Diego returns

Diego the Trapper returned before the first shoots appeared in the garden. He had a new woman with him, but the same introduction. She approached Sky's lodge, because it was the nearest to the entrance of the village. "Halloo," she called. Inside the lodge, Sky heard the call and recognized the situation. He reached for his hunting bow. "Halloo," the woman called again.

Sky stepped out of his lodge with an angry demeanor. "Go away, you bring sickness and trouble! Go away!"

The women spread her hands in an appeal, "That was the other woman. She is no longer with us. We only want to trade for the pelts you have." Diego dangled a shiny stone necklace.

"Go away, before you get hurt!" Sky strung an arrow on his bow. The Trapper understood the immediate threat, and at this close range it would be deadly.

The woman hesitated before following the retreating Diego. She called loud enough for some of the other lodges to hear, "If you want to trade your pelts, we will be at the stream." As Sky raised his bow, she loped after the Trapper, who was safely out of sight.

At the Long House, Thunder had heard the shouting, and came to investigate. He watched the four hunters who had pelts, stroll down the trail. "Be very careful of their shadow," Thunder cautioned. "And place the necklace in steaming water to kill the illness that might be on it." He really didn't know what else might be said.

Shortly, the hunters returned to the village, holding their trophies proudly. One had two prizes, a red and a white necklace; the others carried either a red, a green or a bright blue one. The other hunters of the village had spent much of the winter braiding their own snares, so they might have something to trade when next the Trapper appeared. Little did any one realize that they had been infected by a much more sinister challenge, the gnawing craving of avarice. This simple beginning would lead to much heartache.

New Arrivals

On the other hand, there were arrivals that brought happy hearts. The hunting canoe from the Salish brought Knapper, his woman, and Sky's little brother, Feather. Three days later it brought the Inuit named Chuiku, and his woman and family. With them was a one-eyed son, who when he saw Thunder, immediately knelt, and through tears, again repented for trying to steal from him. While Thunder tried to lift him to his feet, completely embarrassed by the meeting, the Kwakiutl men who witnessed the greeting marveled, only adding to the legend of their Shaman. They had never before seen someone kneel before a man so reverently.

The Inuit tried to explain, "Since becoming our son, he has told us several times of how he tried to steal your walking stick, and you treated him with sternness, but great compassion. We have given him the new name 'Tswulit.'"

Sky, who had listened to the greeting with much interest, asked, "Isn't that the Inuit word for 'Hawk'?" When assured that it was the same, Sky smiled broadly. "Do you mind if we use our Kwakiutl, 'Hawk'? It will be easier for him to be known." The newcomers chose lodge sites near Sky's, close to the trail and stream. They felt it was a most ideal location, and a very cordial beginning.

The peaceful days of spring gave way to the lazy days of summer. With ample food and no immediate challenges, the village was a picture of tranquility. One afternoon two hunter friends began a discussion of who in the village was the best bowman. At first they had argued their own skill, but soon recalled others who were also very accurate. Finally, they sought Thunder's help in holding a contest.

Fourteen of the village hunters wanted to participate. They agreed to make their arrows a bit longer to compensate for the absence of a stone arrowhead. Spring had woven a target from corn leaves; it had the shape and size of a deer, with a charcoal circle about as large as a fist. Placed against a cleared sand bank near the trail, the archers had a fair contest. Each would shoot four arrows from a distance of thirty strides.

With much discussion and laughter, each man had a try. They all hit the woven outline; four of the archers had two arrows in the black circle. Those four were moved ten strides further from the target, and launched three more arrows. Once again they all hit the woven form, but only Sky had all three of his arrows in the black circle. Amid the loud applause, it was suggested that he teach the nine and ten year old boys how to develop skill with a bow. Thunder offered to teach them to use a sling at the same time. A good natured rivalry had begun that would serve the hunters for years to come.

Sadness for Singing Bird

Before the corn harvest, a tragedy shook the village. A group of hunters had put the large log canoe into service. They had managed to bring in several seals, which would mean an even more abundant food source for the winter. On a cloudy day they had drifted near a rock where a Sea lion was resting. Two powerful spear thrusts had delivered mortal wounds, but the animal was able to surge into the water. In their attempt to secure the massive hulk to the boat, they had made the mistake of all ten standing on one side of the boat, which caused it to capsize enough to throw them all into the cold water. Not until they had scrambled back into the boat did they realize that only nine of them were safe. In the turmoil Antler, a young hunter, had been thrown backwards, hitting his head and neck. He never resurfaced. His woman, Singing Bird had an infant son who would never get to know his father.

"Thunder, may I ask you a question?" Slow Bear was preparing for another story time.

"Of course," his friend replied. "What is it?"

"Near my lodge is that of the young widow, Singing Bird. She must tend the infant without help from a family, and every night I listen to her sobbing. It is a very sad sound." He paused, trying to decide how to ask such a personal question. "I've wondered since you live here alone, could you bring her here as your woman? She is about your age, and her weeping is painful to hear." His earnestness got ahead of his practicality. "You were gracious enough to give me shelter when I had no one. Perhaps you could help her too." As he said it, he realized how preposterous his request sounded.

Thunder let his hand rest on the shoulder of this good friend. "It is because your heart cares for our village that you ask. It is a fine question. She has no man to care for her or her child. As I think on it there are no men who might take her into their lodge. But without fondness, this lodge would be as empty as the one she is in now." There was stillness for a bit until he said, "But you have a reason to be concerned about her. Who will provide her meat for the winter, or wood for the fire. You are right, she needs someone's help." As a smile played at the edge of his mouth, Thunder added, "Perhaps when you deliver her share of the corn field, you might offer to help her prepare it for drying, and offer to bring a bit of wood when you gather your next armful." It was a seed that could grow into a powerful thought.

Surplus Food

The red fish reappeared, more numerous than usual. The canoe, and capturing basket, was busy for almost a moon. Many of the women worked to clean and cut into strips the flesh that would be dried and stored. Their bounty, when added to the deer and seal strips, was more than their storage space could hold. The council decided to add a lodge beside the Long House that would be used to keep the excess. No one could recall a more bountiful time. It was simple, therefore, to suggest that Slow Bear should receive a bit of the hunt for his work with the children. He was given the front shoulder of several deer, which he happily shared with a young grateful widow. They filled a drying rack with strips.

When it was time to harvest the squash, Slow Bear was again happy to show Singing Bird how to open the large fruit, save the seeds, and chop the flesh into dryable portions. Before the winter rains set in he asked her if she would move into his lodge. She countered that hers was more spacious, and he could use his to store the bags of seeds for next year's garden. It may have been an unusual arrangement, but no one could argue the practicality of it.

It was also one of those late fall mornings when Hawk came to Thunder, reporting that he had seen three strangers on the trail from the waterfall. "I think they were speaking Haida, and they were trying to hide in the brush when they heard me coming." Hawk was sharing important information with the only person he could think of that would do something about it.

"Perhaps they have heard what a generous village we have," Thunder said with a grin. "If they come openly as friends, we will welcome them as guests. If they have other plans, perhaps we can teach them not to do that." He stopped at a lodge, speaking momentarily with a youth there, and asking him to pass the message to the others. "Let's go up to the Long House and keep watch, as a Hawk might," A chuckle punctuated the humor he felt. They were there only briefly before four lads joined them, each carrying a simple sling and a pouch filled with rocks about the size of a nut. They were about the same age as Hawk, and responding to the request Thunder had made for their help.

"I call these young men 'Wasps,'" he announced happily. "They were the best of the students who learned to use the sling." Poking Hawk fondly, Thunder said, "And you can remember how effective the sting of a sling can be." Thunder explained to the boys that some strangers had been seen on the trail, "and they might be sneaking into our village with bad intent. Let's keep watch for a while." All five lads felt honored to be given the task of protecting their home and village.

The sun was trying to battle through the clouds directly overhead when Hawk touched Thunder's arm, pointing toward the far end of the garden. All the crops had been harvested, but there was enough debris and stalks to give a bit of cover. They watched the three figures crouch down surveying the village. They moved a little closer to the hill and paused again, their heads close in conversation. Once again they scuttled along the foot of the hill, finding another hiding place.

"I think they are almost in your range. Do you remember to aim high so your stones will fall like rain," Thunder whispered. "Once you start, cast all your stones. If they are not enough, we can call to the hunters with their bows for protection." The three sneaking forms scurried a bit closer. There was a mischievous twinkle in Thunder's eye as he asked, "Are you ready for your first defense?"

The smiling faces all nodded, but there was a tremble common to them all.

"Get them!" Thunder said quietly. They understood; stepping to the edge of the Long House ridge silently, spaced apart enough to swing their slings and launch a barrage of stones, they were a formidable force. It took a few heartbeats before the crouching three realized they were under attack. They looked around to find their assailants, then one was hit by a stone and screamed in pain. A second joined him. More stones pelted down. The first victim was hit again and squealed as he began to run for the distant shelter of the trees. Another howled as a rock bounced off his back. They were all hit repeatedly, and in full retreat. Finally, Thunder stood and joined the flight of stones with some of his own. He calculated that he had a bit more distance in his throws, so he aimed where the retreating forms were heading. One fell momentarily stunned, and a second screamed again. Then they were lost in the shadows and shelter of the woods.

"Good shooting, Wasps," Thunder said with obvious satisfaction, and more than a little affection. "Now go tell your fathers that we have had some unwanted visitors. They might want to make sure that the three are really gone from our village." He gave Hawk a special pat on the back. "Thank you for your watchfulness. We needed a guard, and you did it well." The future would prove the truth of those words.

The three intruders didn't slow down until they reached their beached boat. They had heard of the generosity of the Kwakiutl village, and misunderstood its meaning. They were looking for women for easy pleasure, and were still mystified at the cause of their painful injuries. As the story was told and retold, the assault grew more sinister. Any listener would wonder how they had escaped alive. It was finally circulated that the Kwakiutl village was guarded by Taghil, for they did feel the earth tremble and the mystical trickster had dealt severely with them, pelting them with hundreds of rocks. Had Taghil used larger stones, they would surely have perished.

Abundant Harvest

The garden area gave the village a new time schedule of duties. The dried leaves and vines left after a harvesting, were carefully gathered and burned before the red fish reappeared; that seemed to be the first season of preparation. Then the refuse from cleaning the fish was buried along the growing rows. That was the second beat of the singing drum of their garden song. The ground rested until the planting time. The careful distribution of new seeds along straight rows was as exact as possible. That was the mystery of their future success. Protection was needed to keep out deer, squirrels and crows that would feed on the growing plants. Finally there was the joy of the harvest and tending the drying of the food. Each process a step in the turning seasons, which became a rhythm of peace. There was still much hunting that needed to happen of course; the garden, however, redefined the Kwakiutl village into a more coordinated activity, and gave their story a happy song.

An early snow draped the village in a blanket of stillness. Most of the folks stayed inside, near the fire. The hunters who needed to check their snares were bold enough to retrace their paths hopefully, and when Slow

Bear packed the trail up to the Long House, the children were delighted by an entire morning of storytelling.

In a very few days the rains returned, turning the snow first to sloppy slush, and then mud. Still the hunters tended their snares. One brought back a Bobcat, and another announced that for a moment he had captured a bear. Fortunately for him only the snare was torn to pieces. The winter passed slowly, but predictably.

When the days began to lengthen, Slow Bear devised a way to clear one more row for the garden. The production of corn seemed limitless. Thunder took the canoe across the big water to spend a moon with the Haida village. The fondness that he was feeling for the young woman named Breath made the days hurry by like butterflies. The Haida had heard the account of three young men seeking night play that had instead been rained upon by Taghil's stones. They remembered how six Salish had also felt "Taghil's" wrath. Thunder said nothing that would lessen the story or his village's reputation. They also told Thunder about the trouble they had with a Trapper from the outside. He had tried to cheat the hunters on the value of their pelts, and he had finally been forcibly removed from the village when he abused a man's woman.

By the time Thunder returned to the Kwakiutl village, it was nearing time to plant. He received two happy pieces of news. Slow Bear had organized enough planters to get the entire field planted in one day. The second news was much better; Sky was to become a father. Somehow both announcements made the Shaman very glad, but emancipated from his obligation to the village. He was sure they could get along without him. When the Trapper returned, he saw how true those feelings were.

Outrageous Business

"Halloo!" The voice was different, but Sky's response was the same. "Halloo! Are there hunters who want to.." Her words were cut off by an angry Sky who stepped out of his lodge holding his hunting bow.

"Go away! We don't want your sickness. You have nothing we want!" He gestured with his bow to punctuate the point.

"Please listen" the woman said in desperation. She was speaking Haida. It was then that Sky noticed the bruises on her arms and face. "My name is Fawn. He will be very angry with me if I do not get you to trade your pelts." She was near tears, and old enough to be Sky's mother, maybe older. The Trapper growled something to her that made her shake her head. "He says he will trade a necklace for four good pelts. He doesn't want inferior ones." She looked at the ground unable to meet Sky's angry stare.

Once again the Trapper growled at her, and raised his hand to strike her. She cowered away, quickly saying, "He insists you bring the pelts down to the waterfall before sunset." She ducked and scurried back down the trail away from the village, the man striding behind her.

That information did not sit well with the hunters who had worked all winter to gather and cure the pelts under the impression they could trade two for one necklace. Sky reported the changes of the trade to Thunder and as many council members as he could find. A fairly surly crowd finally gathered to make the delivery. Thunder was happy to see that no one carried a weapon. Within a short while, he might feel differently about that.

The sun was still high in the sky when they arrived at the waterfall. The Trapper stood by his canoe, which already had a decent pile of pelts. He barked instructions that Fawn immediately translated. "He will grade the pelts one at a time." The aggressive attitude of the Trapper was in control of the situation.

The first hunter brought his armful of pelts. "That's a good one," the Trapper said, but shook his head on the next two. "No good!" Yet he tossed the pelts onto the acceptable pile in his canoe. "That's a good one; so is that. No good." But again the rejected pelt went in with the others. That's a good one, but that last one is no good." He held up one necklace as compensation to the hunter. "Here's your prize," he spoke in a language no one could understand. "Take the necklace!" he jabbed it at the hunter, who then shook his head holding up three fingers.

Hawk had made his way to Thunder's side, where he could whisper, "He's speaking Inuit to her, telling her to cheat us or he will beat her again." Thunder could feel the young man tense as though ready to leap into the action. A cautioning hand held him back. "These men do not need our protection, yet," was whispered in response.

Another hunter's pelts were being examined, with the same results. Half were deemed acceptable and the rest rejected, but thrown into the Trapper's canoe. Once again one necklace was offered. The crowd was becoming agitated. The Trapper barked at the woman, who replied something under her breath, and was clubbed on the side of her head hard enough to buckle her knees. She held on to the side of the canoe for support. Once again the command was given, and she shook her head, Once again the hand raised to strike her, but a diminutive Hawk threw himself at the larger man, growling like an angry animal. The blow that started at the woman struck the boy on the back of the head rendering him unconscious. That's when the fist end of Thunder's walking stick struck the Trapper in the forehead. The head snapped back and the eyes rolled up as the large man also fell, oblivious to the world. Finally Sky joined the scene. There was much confusion and stunned surprise at Thunder's instant and powerful response.

Fawn who was weeping, said through sobs, "He bought me from the Skookumchuck Chief for two necklaces. My husband died two summers ago. I have no children and no man, so I was claimed by the Chief as his slave. This is a very bad man. He has made many sick, and hurt many more. Nothing he says is true." Her tears ran down wet cheeks.

Hawk was feebly trying to rise to his feet. When he saw the blood covered face of the Trapper, he asked, "Did I do that?" It was incongruous enough to break the moment open so a plan could form.

Thunder asked Sky if he could take the Trapper's canoe, with Fawn. "Paddle upstream on this fork of the river," it was one they had not explored, "until you are out of sight completely. We will tell the Trapper that Fawn has gone back to her village to give back the pelts." He reached down and relieved the Trapper of the fistful of necklaces that he still held. Giving them to the hunters who had been offered so little, he said, "You can make a fair division of these."

Moments after Sky had disappeared around the river bend, the Trapper's eyes opened. With a groan he touched the ragged wound on his forehead. He managed to stagger to his feet, then looking about, he muttered a question.

Hawk, who was standing a safe distance away, translated, "He wants to know where his canoe might be, and the woman." The folks standing nearby, shuffled a bit further from the Trapper, who asked the same question in a louder voice.

Thunder was about to tell Hawk what to say in answer, but the young one eyed boy stepped closer to the man jabbering in Inuit, and pointing toward the big water. He waved his arm as though indicating the direction she may have gone.

The man said he had noticed the village had a canoe. "I will use it to catch the woman," he said, assuming authority no one had offered. Hawk translated for Thunder, who promptly denied the suggestion.

Striding toward the canoe that was safely in its place, the man said, "Then I will take it!" Suddenly he pulled a most unusual blade from a leather holder at his waist. Hawk saw the threat, and shouted a warning. The blade looked thin and weak, but it had the sheen of frozen water.

One of the hunters named Ram stepped in front of the Trapper, blocking his way toward the canoe. The circle of villagers tightened around the Trapper in defense of their prized possession. In a shout of rage, the Trapper's hand swung in a vicious arc, dragging the blade across Ram's shoulder and chest. Instantly the hide shirt parted and the blood was evident that he had been seriously wounded. A gasp escaped from the crowd, but just as suddenly Thunder's walking stick flew into action. It was the only available weapon. The sharp pointed end was thrust at the shoulder of the man, much as he had thrust at the attacking Salish so long ago. This time the thrust was meant to disable instantly. The Trapper reeled away from the pain, but the long lance device followed him in his backward stagger. He lost his footing and collapsed in a pile of anger and frustration, the point of the stick well embedded in his flesh. His arms spread wide in surrender, and the blade slipped from his hand. As quickly as the struggle had begun, it was over.

"Tell him to lie still, or he will lose the use of his arm forever," Thunder spoke softly to Hawk. When the words were translated the man nodded in understanding. He didn't move.

Sky returned on foot from his task just in time. It only took him a moment to understand the situation. Thunder was explaining to the Trapper what was going to happen. "We will take you back to our village. There is a trail that will lead you to the Sechelt village. From there you may go two or three days farther to the Skookumchucks. Perhaps you will find your canoe and pelts there, or perhaps she has taken the pelts back to the Haida." Hawk was faithfully translating Thunder's words.

Thunder added, "The first time you came to our village, you brought a terrible sickness. This time you bring disrespect and trouble. You are no longer welcome with the Kwakiutl. We want you to never come here again." Once again Hawk translated the words, but added his own anger to them.

The man started to argue, saying he had no food, nor anything to trade. Before Hawk could translate for Thunder, Sky bent down and snarled, "You are lucky to be able to walk out of here at all. If I ever smell your bad breath or stinking body, I will plant you under the ground myself." There was no further discussion.

Thunder removed the point of the walking stick from his shoulder and told the man to take off his shirt. With the unusual blade, Thunder cut the front of Ram's hide shirt so they could remove it from his bloody chest. It really was an ugly wound. The Trapper was unbuttoning his shirt, which was something of a marvel to the villagers. Thunder threw Ram's cut and soiled shirt at the Trapper, saying, "You destroyed Ram's shirt, now he will wear yours." As Hawk translated there was nearly a giggle of justice in his voice.

The Trapper cast the bloody leather shirt aside, saying he would not put that on.

"Suit yourself," Thunder replied casually. "The night will be cold and you have no other robe. We really don't care." Then speaking to the villagers around him, he said, "Stand him up, but do not release him until we get to our village." The Trapper was something of a mess with a jagged tear on his forehead that had bled freely down his face, and a puncture in his shoulder that brought a curse every time his arm was jerked. He grabbed the hide shirt at the last moment. For him it was a long bumpy walk back up the hill. Finally, at the rapids, Thunder said to him, "Wade across here, and go straight ahead until you come to the trail. If we ever see you again, we will kill you like a common prowler." It was nearing sunset, and his journey would be trying at best. With a shove, Thunder set him floundering through the cold water.

Another Generosity

The next morning, Sky and Hawk retraced their steps to the waterfall, and then through the brush until they found Fawn. She said it was the best rest she could remember; she had extra robes for warmth, ample food, and no mean man shouting at her. A warm smile was her gift to the morning. Sky noticed a soft breeze rustling the new leaves

When they unloaded the canoe, they were surprised to find four bales of pelts; far more than they expected. Sky and Hawk could carry those, if Fawn could manage the robes and gathering bags. All three were grateful when they finally entered the village and proceeded directly to the Long House. Thunder greeted Fawn, and shared that the council was to meet after the mid day meal. They had business to discuss. The smile on his face suggested that it might be good business.

When the Elders had gathered they were happy to see that as usual, Thunder had prepared steaming cup. He even offered one to young Hawk, and to Fawn. The breeze felt pleasant in the warm spring afternoon. Finally, Chief Bear asked Thunder why they were called together. The unusual deference to their Shaman was not missed by any of them.

Thunder had a wide smile as he said to the council, "This is my home. Sometimes we have hard days, like yesterday, and sometimes we have very happy days like today." He looked at the faces he knew as well as family. "Today I want to make a suggestion that will improve our village, and serve our council well." Everyone was interested of course, but could not imagine what their Shaman had in mind.

"We have an extraordinary young man in our village who has displayed courage beyond his years. Hawk is his name, and you know him as part of the new Inuit lodge that has moved here. I would like the council to approve some special training for Hawk in hunting skills and tracking. I am hoping that he will become our Guardian, working with the other four young men I call 'Wasps.' Together they can be a shield of security for our village so we may never again be bothered by Trappers. I think we could be grooming the next generation of Elders." There followed some discussion, but the subject was far from urgent. Finally, when the Chief asked for "Palms up," a unanimous vote was cast.

"Secondly," Thunder said more slowly, "we have an opportunity to act like a village with wisdom and compassion." The councilmen exchanged glances for again they had no idea where this was going. "The Trapper bought a slave from the Skookumchuck Chief. She was a woman whose husband lost his life in the big water, fishing. She had no family to protect her, so the Chief claimed her, and then sold her for two necklaces to the Trapper. You know the rest; you saw his terrible treatment. She still has bruises. I am suggesting that we allow her to live in our village, not as my woman, or Chief Bear's, but as this Long House's, where she will live. She will help clean and cut the red fish strips with everyone else. She will cut strips of deer and seal, as well as prepare the food from our garden for drying. She will guard our supplies when I am not here, and she will prepare steaming cups for the council meeting. I can even teach her how to prepare the smoking pipe for you. She will be safe here, not for the use of night play, unless she wants it." A snicker was shared, even by the woman standing outside the entrance. We will treat her as our mother. She can give help in childbearing." Thunder realized he was getting too descriptive, and hoped that he had said enough. There was no discussion about the matter, so the Chief asked for "Palms up." Once again it was unanimous.

"One last thing, Chief," Thunder said with a shrug. "We must decide what should be done with the pelts and necklaces from the Trapper. He tried to steal from us, and I believe he found justice here. There is the matter of many pelts and trinket's, not to mention his canoe. I have only a suggestion that should be discussed. If we were to host a Potlatch after the garden is harvested, we could give all this to the people who attend. We know that he stole much from the Haida village, but who knows where else. I think it would not be just for us to keep it all for ourselves, although we could all use the canoe.

The council unanimously agreed.

Thunder slid the Trapper's blade, safe in its leather holder, in front of the Chief. There was something sinister about it, for it looked innocent, but was mysteriously dangerous. He had no way of knowing that it's kind would be the undoing of their way of life. "Our Chief must be the keeper of this most unusual blade." The Iron Age had just arrived at the Kwakiutl village.

Thunder knew he was overdue for a walk in the wind.

Finis: Book Three: Unexpected Wealth

Book 4

Defense of the Nation

Table of Contents

Like Children Dancing

The seasons follow one another like children dancing. Leaders are replaced by those who are younger, stronger, and hopefully wiser. Chief Blade of the Haida died in his sleep. After a lengthy discussion, Klaw was named Chief. Chief Otter of the Salish was wounded in a skirmish with Traders; after several days of fever, he stopped breathing. Arrow, his son, a strong warrior, became the new Chief. Chief Bear of the Kwakiutl suffered a paralysis of his speech, and then his right arm and leg. He lived long enough to help the council see that Sky was his obvious successor. Chief Storm Cloud of the Sechelt had been given bottled medicine water by a Trapper several times. The strong water clouded his judgment, and made him act like a fool. He became an embarrassment to the village and was finally replaced by a young hunter, who was a careful leader. Spear, Fawn, and Basket had gone to be with the Ancients like many others. Thunder took a lodge in the Haida village with Breath, who, in time, gave birth to three sons and a daughter. The Shaman to the First Nation visited the villages of the Sechelt, Salish and Kwakiutl regularly. Yes, seasons follow one another like children dancing.

The wind had blown steady from the Morning Mountains for seven days. It was a very bad sign that interrupted an otherwise perfect springtime. Thunder went to Chief Klaw's lodge to talk with Helps. Her hair had turned white, and there were wrinkles on her face, perhaps gifts from her large family. Her eyes, though, seemed timeless, sparkling with youth and knowledge. She said, "I don't know the reason. But if your heart tells you that trouble is nearby, I do trust that. What shall we do?" Her genuine affection for him was a constant source of strength.

"I must go across to the Sechelt village and talk with them," Thunder mused. "We've known trouble from the Outsiders, but it has never troubled the wind. I think this must be different." Thunder's trust in the wind's guidance was legendary. He had very rarely misread the wind's message.

Thunder said farewell to his family, promising to return soon. Regrettably, that promise would take almost a year to keep. With his walking stick, a robe for shelter and a gathering bag with enough deer strips and corn cakes for eight days, he left, walking up the same hill that he and Sky had climbed so very long ago. He smiled, thinking that the trail should be called "Not Know." They did not know where they were bound the first time they climbed this gentle grade, and he did not know what the future held for any of his people.

It took Thunder only five days to reach Nanoose Bay, where his canoe was hidden. He had avoided the Salish village, because the last time he visited, he had been unwelcomed there. Chief Arrow had accused the Kwakiutl of stealing lodges from them. He was so discourteous, Thunder had been unable to help them in any way, and left when assailed by much name-calling.

The canoe was light and slipped easily across the water, although today the wind had agitated the waves directly in Thunder's path. The water was going out, which could be of some help to him, but the journey would be slower because of the waves. He knew the way to Slow Bear's deserted village. The sun was sliding through the afternoon sky when he finally managed to hide his canoe at the overgrown site. The trail to the Sechelt village had been traveled enough to be easy to find.

A Tragic Story

The village seemed agitated to Thunder as he made his way to the Long House. Gone was the jovial friendliness he remembered. At the Long House a gathering of men recognized him with more enthusiasm. They told him there was great sorrow in a distant Sechelt village where their Great Grandfathers had lived long ago. It was beside the big water, where Outsiders commonly visited. A group of women had arrived two days ago, telling a story of terrible destruction. Chief Heron was with them now if Thunder would like to hear their story.

After the formal introduction, the Chief complimented Thunder for his reputation of mercy to the Sechelt. "My older brother was one whom you cared for when he was severely wounded," the Chief reflected. "Your help may be needed again." He then gave Thunder the report the women had brought.

"It began with one Trapper who came to collect pelts and spread a terrible sickness." Thunder nodded remembering the same thing. "There followed many Traders, looking for pelts, or food, or women for night play." A deep frown on the Chief's face hinted that some of that experience may have been personally painful for his people as well. "They took what had great value, and traded it for what was worthless, or worse, more sickness. At first they offered buttons and thread, even blankets, which were warm. But there were many men who drank the medicine water the Outsiders brought; they traded their senses for it. Many women were contaminated by the traders; they developed sores and seepage. They passed it on to their men. Some have died from it." The Chief shrugged in a quiet despair.

"Last winter, when the Sechelt ran out of food themselves, they finally realized their terrible mistake. A great floating lodge brought many Outside warriors for food. A village man denied them any further trades, and told them to go away. A warrior from the floating lodge wore many buttons, and had a long knife. He struck the man so quickly the blade passed all the way through the man, who died instantly. Many villagers came to chase them away, but the many buttons had smoke sticks that spit death."

"The women told of a night attack by the village men who bravely took bags of burning coals resting in moss. Their intent was to smoke the buttons away as they smoke honey bees. By canoes they went out to the floating lodge and tossed the bags on it, then opened the side vents and tossed more inside. Men with smoke sticks sprayed them with death. Some of the coals, however, that went inside the lodge must have set a fire that grew. When the buttons began spraying the canoes with giant smoke sticks, all the canoes were destroyed, and the men in them. Then the fire inside grew suddenly, a huge cloud of smoke and fire sounded like thunder, with splinters of wood flying all the way to the shore. All the buttons were killed too." The account was nearly too large to comprehend.

"The worst was yet to be told, for the day after that an even larger floating lodge, being pulled by clouds, came to the village. It had many giant smoke sticks that spit death on the village. Swarms of sharp rocks and hard twigs (nails) tore through the lodges. Only the ones who could flee into the woods were spared. The air was so filled with smoke it seemed like dense fog to them, except for the screams and crying. When the giant lodge went away, the women returned to see what they could do for their people. Most were dead, or would die soon. A very few were able to make it to the Skookumchuck village, and eleven women came to us, hoping for shelter." The Chief took a deep breath; this was a larger tragedy than he could grasp.

Looking at Thunder, the young Chief said, "I must keep our village safe from such an attack."

The Shaman nodded in agreement. "The Kwakiutl started training young guardians many years ago. It was a way to teach them to hunt and to be excellent marksmen. Their job was to warn the village of Outsiders who might venture in for trading. I'm sure they became the best hunters and strongest councilmen. You might think of a simple start that could grow into a strong defense. Wisdom teaches us that it is better to keep a problem away than rid it once it's established."

"Will you do that for the Sechelt?" the Chief asked recovering from the gloom of the story he had related.

"I am Shaman of the First Nation, so I cannot say 'No,'" Thunder said with a large smile. "But I am also a poor hunter. In our village we had a contest to see who could be the best archer. That's the right one to teach young talent. Why teach them how not to do it? On the other hand, I have used a simple sling to my advantage on several occasions. Is there someone in your village who can use a sling?"

At the end of the conversation Thunder agreed to organize a contest to find the most accurate archer. He would also recruit six youth to be Wasps, junior guardians. He went back to the Long House confident there were enough men there to get the message circulated about a shooting contest. He was also directed to the lodge with the young man most often in trouble. He was the one Thunder would teach to use the sling, and recruit five more to join him.

Seven days later, there was one archer who had been established as the best, and who would teach the young men. There were also seven Wasp starters, who along with three men, had learned to appreciate the skill of the simple sling. Their status became enviable by all the other men when they demonstrated the distance a sling can cast a stone, and when they were also designated by the Chief to be the Guardians.

Swift Justice

From a sound sleep, Thunder was awakened by the shifting wind. A strong breeze from the north rattled the limbs overhead. He knew it to be an omen of warning. With the dawn he was prepared to leave, having given the Chief thanks for the gathering bag with ample deer strips and seed cakes for several days. No one noticed Thunder make his way to the trail heading south toward the Skookumchuck village. Part of the growing aura of the First Nation's Shaman was the mysterious way in which he arrived in a village and took his leave, without ceremony.

He had only been in the Skookumchuck village twice before and those were happy occasions. As he arrived, he could sense this was not such a time; a Trapper had offended them terribly. He stopped at a man's lodge to trade for fine beaver pelts. As they had talked about the trade, the Trapper had given the man a cup of medicine water; then he gave another to the man, and one to his woman. Finally, after a third cup, the Trapper insisted on night play with the woman. When she refused, the Trapper struck her face so violently he knocked her unconscious. He also clubbed the man who was already impaired, under the influence of the medicine water. Then he ravished the woman. When he was finished, he struck her face again out of contempt. He took the pelts leaving nothing but misery and pain.

Thunder came upon a furious mob, which was just underway to catch up with the Trapper. He was carrying a burden of pelts, and they were fueled by rage. It wouldn't be long before they overtook him. Thunder tried to keep up with them. In less than an hour, they came around a bend in the trail to be confronted by the Trapper, holding a smoke stick pointed directly at the dizzy man.

"You got what you deserve, and so did she," the Trapper snarled. At least that's what Thunder understood the broken Salish words to mean. The smoke stick moved more threateningly at the man. Then a flurry of things happened, almost simultaneously. Thunder asked the trapper if he had ever found his boat, which made his head jerk toward the questioner, and away from where the stick was aimed. The Trapper's face was gray and wrinkled, his hair, which stuck out from under a hat, was white and stringy, but Diego was very recognizable. He pulled the trigger on the smoke stick, which gave a puff. The drunken man jerked his head to the side as the smoke stick exploded, singeing his face and ear. The Trapper dropped the smoke stick, and pulled out a shining blade from his waist, lurching a vicious thrust at Thunder.

Perhaps it was planned, and just as possibly it was a recalled response, the walking stick swung up as the Trapper's body attacked. This time Thunder wasn't aiming to disable with a shoulder wound. He drove the point deep into the man's chest. Surprised eyes looked at the lance that had penetrated lethally, the knife slipping from his fingers. In a movement that would be retold forever, Thunder dropped the walking stick to pick up the blade. With one swift stroke he cut the throat of the offensive old man. "I told you if I ever saw you again, I would kill you." He just had. The entire confrontation had happened so fast the others from the village stood still, in shock.

The crowd helped Thunder strip the Trapper of his clothes. Thunder made it clear that the smoke stick and all that went with it were of great interest to him. He placed the knife, now safely back in its leather holder, in his gathering bag. The pelts would be returned to their owner, and all the rest would be distributed by the council, most of whom were standing near him. They put the Trapper's hat on Thunder's head as coup.

When they got back to the village, the men were anxious to go tell the story of the warrior Shaman. Thunder was anxious to see if he could help the woman who had been beaten. She was still in misery, her jaw at an odd angle. The Shaman admitted that he had never tried to realign such a pretty face, but he would try. He placed one hand under her jaw, and the other on the side of her face. "Now this might..." Before he said the next word he pushed solidly on the side of her face, moving her chin, while his other hand was lifting the crook of her jaw bone. They both felt a sharp click as she whimpered a moan. "...hurt a bit," he finished the sentence. She smiled a weak smile that allowed them both to understand that it was realigned. "Now for the nose. You know, I have a wonderful friend whose nose is much like this." He covered her nose with a deer pad that had been soaked in cold water, Placing his fingers along the sides of her nose he simply pressed firmly. Once again they both were aware of the movement of broken bones and repair. "I didn't warn you about that one." Now the woman attempted a little smile. Through tears, she almost made it.

"He will never bother another woman," the Shaman whispered.

"Did you punish him?" she asked just as quietly.

"Severely," was all Thunder could reply. There was still a harsh taste in his mouth. He longed to walk in the wind and explain himself.

Misery

Thunder walked to the Sechelt village that had been laid waste by the giant smoke sticks. It still smelled of bitter smoke and death. He looked into lodges that had been ripped apart by the fury of the floating lodge. There was dried blood everywhere, like Taghil's most terrible tantrum. The women had taken the bodies to the water instead of burying them. There were so many. He could still see shapes in the deep water when it ran out. His practicality had thought to scavenge anything of value, but was overwhelmed with the destruction. Thunder climbed the hill behind the village. From there he should have been able to see the beautiful vista of happy lodges, laughing children and strong men looking out at the water and mountains beyond. Instead, a sob forced its way out of his throat, and he wept for these lost people.

A New Emergency

Thunder was still grieving when he returned to the Skookumchuck village. Seeking the influence of the council, he made his way to the Long House, which was a frequent gathering place. There he learned that the council had met to discuss the matter of the Trapper. They had unanimously applauded Thunder's decisive action, and his treatment of the injured woman as well. He was taken to the Chief's lodge for an introduction.

"Chief Gray Goose, this is the man we told you about. His name is Thunder, Shaman from the Kwakiutl village." The Chief invited Thunder to sit by the lodge fire and they talked about his journey, and his purpose with the Skookumchuck.

"The wind guided me here, Thunder said sincerely. "I was on my way to the Sechelt village to see if there might be anything I could do to help the ones who were injured. Obviously the injuries were beyond help."

"Perhaps the wind had another place in mind," the Chief said softly. "There was a young Outsider here this morning, seeking someone who can speak Haida, at least that's what I was led to believe he wanted. He was not a Trader, but like one, he was dressed strangely."

The Chief asked the men standing nearby if they knew anything more about the Outsider. When they shook their heads, he asked Thunder, "Would you like them to show you where this young man might be?" And so opened another saga that Thunder had never planned, but always welcomed.

In need of a healer

They led him to a wide path that descended toward the water. Obviously it had been well used by many. Huge Big Leaf (Maple) and other trees hung over the trail like a canopy roof. At the bottom of the hill, Thunder could see the gravel of a beach. When they made their way out onto that beach, he realized it was part of a sheltered cove, with barrier rocks giving protection from the big water. Resting in the cove was a large floating lodge, with bare trees standing on it. A small canoe was pulled up on the gravel and sitting on that was a young man who reminded Thunder of his first meeting with Slow Bear. His face was drawn in worry and sadness. He looked up at their arrival.

"Praise God, you have found someone to speak Haida!" he said hopping toward them. Thunder had understood only the last word spoken.

He guessed the man's age as fourteen or fifteen summers. He had unruly hair the color of the Fox, his eyes were the color of soft blue water, white skin with many brown spots, and a huge smile. Without knowing why, Thunder liked this young Outsider.

"Do you speak Haida?" the man asked. His words were poor, but Thunder understood, so he nodded and said, "I speak Haida and all the other languages of the First Nation."

There was a quizzical smile on the man's face, for he had not understood all of Thunder's words, but enough to believe they could communicate.

"Praise God!" he said again in a language that Thunder did not understand. In broken Haida, he asked, "Those with me are very sick, all of them. Yesterday, they all became" he rubbed his stomach, bottom, and then made a sign of vomiting. If the words failed, showing the distress worked. Thunder nodded in understanding.

"Did your people eat fish, or drink bad water?" He tried to make the words simple and slow.

"Yes, they ate clams, and took on fresh water." A puzzle drifted across his face.

Thunder asked again for clarity, "Is their sickness," he rubbed his stomach "not chest," he rubbed his chest and coughed? When it was confirmed that the sickness was abdominal, Thunder asked, "But why didn't you get sick? Did you not eat the clams?"

The lad grinned saying, "I don't like fish of any sort. I have only been eating bread and cheese." Again the words were broken, but Thunder, using the words he could understand, encouraged him that they could be helped.

Joining in the smile, Thunder said, "I ate bad clams once and thought I was near death. I believe we can help your people. How many are in your lodge?"

"It's called a ship," the lad corrected. Thunder repeated the new word. "There are thirty two, counting the officers." Again his words were a mix of Haida and Outsider.

"Do you speak Haida?" Thunder asked, this time with little humor.

Yes, I'm sorry," he spoke once again with the correct words. "I am happy to be able to speak with you." He was speaking like a child, but it would work.

"Did you drink the new water?" Thunder asked.

"Yes, I did, it did not hurt me." Again the words were correct but immature.

Turning to the villagers with him, Thunder asked, "Do you know Biting Bush, Caps, Happy leaf or Happy?" They shook their heads in confusion. "Then take my walking stick and put it with the smoke stick in the Long House. I will collect them after I help this man on his floating lodge." The incredulous expression on their face told Thunder they were not supportive of his choice at the moment.

Turning back to the young man, Thunder said in Haida, "My name is Thunder. It will take me only a short while to collect the leaves that will help your people." True to his word, Thunder found the hillside rich in leaves he needed. He even found two Smokes, which would be welcome additions.

With some trepidation Thunder, carrying his full gathering bags, stepped into the different canoe. It was made of wood, and was very solid. He asked, "Do you have enough bread for everyone to have some."

"O Christ, yes!" the happy young man answered. "It may be stale, but it's not moldy."

"In Haida, if you want to speak to me." Thunder cautioned

"Yes, we have bread, maybe old, but still edible." The words were close to correct. The young man was pushing the canoe away from the shore. He waded until they were free, then hopped in agilely. He sat on a brace, taking a paddle in each hand. Like a flapping duck, the paddles worked together, and they moved smoothly toward the floating lodge. Thunder wondered if it had been wise for him to admit his knowledge of Haida.

The Explorers

As Thunder cautiously stepped onto the deck, his eyes, ears and nose were busy absorbing information. He had never imagined such a "ship"; he remembered the word. Wood planks, lines, hatches that lead to lower levels were all mysteries. The silence of the craft led him to believe that the thirty two lives aboard were in desperate condition; there was no moaning. The smell was the familiar rank stench of waste and vomit. The floor beneath his feet was stable and still.

The lad stood beside him, and asked, "What can I do?" in acceptable Haida.

"Can you make fire for hot water?" It was the best place to start. "We must make them healing drink." Before he turned away, Thunder asked, "What name shall I call you?"

The smile returned, "My name is Alexander Boxer." He gave a salute that meant nothing to Thunder.

"'Xander' is a big name. What does it mean?" He gazed again into those blue eyes.

"It means I am the lowest of the crew, They call me a Boson's mate." When Thunder shook his head in confusion, Xander said, "Lowest, not very important."

"Today you are very important," Thunder said as he placed his hand on the strong shoulder. He was drawn to the touch of a fabric shirt, smooth and soft. "Today you are the one who will bring them back from the shadows of sickness. Now make hot water. I will prepare the leaves."

While the iron pot was heating over the galley fire, they explored the ship. Five officers were semiconscious. They did not acknowledge their presence. Down more stairs they found many men lying on mats on the floor. "These are the ones we must get up into the sunlight," Thunder ordered. "You take feet, I'll take hands." One by one the deck was soon filled with quiet patients. Thunder placed the leaves in the water as soon as it started to steam. He found another shiny blade in the galley and very carefully sliced the Smoke into tiny pieces. They went into the warming broth too.

"Get a drinking pouch. We will start with a tiny swallow of steaming wellness for each one. Then we can make stale bread pieces wet with steaming juice. If they swallow the soft cake, they will be able to receive fresh water. By that time, they will be waking." He said it with enough confidence that Xander knew it was to be.

Xander produced a cup from the galley; he asked, "Is this a 'drinking pouch?'"

Thunder held it carefully, examining all sides. "Very good pouch."

Smiling, the sailor said, "We call it a 'cup.'" They began their procedure, one at a time at first, and then they became a team, each with a purpose. After the first sip of warm broth, the patients received a small sop of bread soaked in the mixture. There was occasional gagging or coughing, but it was seen as a good sign. The sickness was losing its grip. The officers were given a bit larger portion, and seemed to revive more quickly. By sunset, the iron pot had been filled a third time, and there were some of the Outsiders who were able to drink the cup by themselves.

Thunder patted the weary shoulder of the Xander, saying, "You worked very hard. Good Shaman. You can take me back to land," he pointed to the beach where they had met. "I will make my way to the Long House for sleep."

"You are welcome to stay here for the night." Xander was sincere in his desire to continue time spent with this fascinating native. "We have clean blankets that you may spread," he looked around a completely filled deck. "up on the quarterdeck," he said brightly. "There won't be anyone there but you."

"And the wind," Thunder thought. He accepted the offer.

It was not a quiet night, for sure. Thunder was aware of much urination and runny waste somewhere behind him, and the clumping of hard shoes on the wooden floor, He was also aware of the soft wind reminding him to listen, and learn. The wind gave him encouragement, for he knew that in this alien place, he was not alone. The wind was with him. He dozed comfortably.

The sun was still waking behind the Morning Mountains when Thunder sat up, listening to the sounds of sea birds and men climbing out of the sleep. By the evidence, he knew that they were recovering from the illness. Suddenly from right behind him a loud clanging sound repeated, and repeated. Much later, he would learn to identify the sound as a warning bell. Thunder covered his ears in discomfort from the piercing sound. A voice was calling. Then harsh hands grabbed him, thrust him down to the floor on his stomach and pulled his hands behind him. A heavy knee was pressed in his back to hold him down. He was careful not to struggle or put up any resistance that might escalate into war. The calling voice was still babbling.

"There's a savage on board! I got the little bugger! Be still Chief or I will put you out of your misery," were the babbling words which Thunder could not understand A breeze rippled across the cove, and Thunder tried to relax even more.

"For Christ sake, Rifkin, you Dublin Dummy, did your mother have any children with a brain? Let go of that man! You horse's arss, he's the reason you are up and breathin' this morning! Damn your ignorance!" Xander barged onto the quarterdeck through the knot of Outsiders, who were now staring at Thunder, and beginning to understand the drama that had taken place in yesterday's afternoon and evening. Thunder was helped up by an apologetic friend. In Haida, he said, "Please forgive these children. They have been very sick." The smile that bloomed on his ruddy face was evidence his words were true. A shrill whistle startled him again, as two men in different clothes joined the crowd. The others stood stiffly and made way. Thunder assumed these were Chiefs of the lodge. Xander was speaking rapidly in his babble to them. There was babbling in return, and Xander's countenance fell. He shrugged and turned to Thunder.

"The Chief is very happy for your help in making the ship well. He says we want a translator. He wants you to stay with us." Xander's troubled face was matched by Thunder's expression.

"My lodge is with the Haida, but I am Shaman to the First Nation." He pointed northwest, "To the Haida." His hand swept around to the south west and southeast,

"To the Salish," Then to the northeast, "to the Kwakiutl, and up to the ice, to the Inuit. I cannot stay on this chip." He mispronounced the word. There was more babbling between the Outsiders.

Xander hesitated before telling Thunder, "He says that's all well and good, but we need you to translate. You must come with us." The wind in the cove was still.

"Xander," Thunder replied softly, "I helped you with sickness because I do not want to be at war with Outsiders. But I am not a night play woman that you can take, nor a slave that has no choice. Please tell your Chief that as easily as you all were made well, I can make you sick, or worse. Two days ago a Trapper named Diego thought he could take what he wanted. He thought he could insult us, and I cut his throat. Please tell your Chief that I will help when I can, but this morning you are going to take me back to that beach." Thunder pointed to make sure there was no confusion.

A Smoke Stick

Much babbling followed. When Thunder heard the name Diego, and the babbling that followed, a change happened to the men around him. They shuffled a bit away. Thunder thought perhaps they were in respect for him, or some fear, or both. The Chief's voice softened, and he spoke once more to Xander,

"The Chief is grateful for your help with our illness, and apologizes for any disrespect. May we offer something for your kindness?" The wind returned from the west, a good sign. As Thunder looked at this young man with blue eyes, he thought of his friend Sky. Now it was a good morning. "You have nothing of value to me," Thunder said softly. He didn't want to insult this friend. "But there is one thing." He hesitated, then decided to ask anyway. "I have never seen a smoke stick. Can you demonstrate one for me?"

There was more babbling, then laughter. The Chiefs turned and walked away. Xander reported, "Chief says usually when rifle," Thunder understood the new word, "is used, people part as enemies. He is happy this is not for us. We want to be your friends." A long smoke st...rifle was brought to Xander. He handled it with wisdom, demonstrating how a dark power was poured in the open end, then a small patch was placed over it and a round object was laid on the patch. Perhaps it was to keep it clean. A long stick pressed the round object into the end and drove it all the way down. Smiling, Xander pulled a branch back with a click, then poured a tiny bit of the dark powder in a cup. While all this was going on, Thunder noticed two or three of the Outsiders were having a smoke pipe by themselves. Xander said in Haida, "Now it will shoot. Are you ready?" When Thunder nodded, the rifle was raised to Xander's shoulder, and in just a moment, there was a white puff of smoke, and then a loud clap of thunder. Three bow shots away, a spout of water showed where the object had hit. The Outsiders were chuckling at Thunder's big startle. He smiled weakly, now aware of how powerful this smo..rifle was, and how dangerous. He needed to walk in the wind and think on all of this.

He said quietly to Xander, "That is the smell of the Sechelt village that giant smoke sticks destroyed. It is only an empty place of death now.

"I am very sorry that happened. The Spaniards are quick to think they own this place."

"Are they from a different tribe of Outsider?" Thunder asked in obvious confusion. It was difficult to imagine more than one tribe of Outsider at a time.

New Path

On the way back to the beach Thunder asked the word for this canoe. Xander said, "It's a boat."

"And the paddles?" the curious passenger wanted to know.

"These are called 'oars,;" he was told.

"There were men using the smoke pipe by themselves." Thunder left the statement open, not sure what he was asking.

"Yes, they were smoking. Many of us do that, but not as a ceremony." Xander hoped he had said enough.

"We use the smoke pipe at the council meeting. For us it is a time for prayer, a happy time to remember." Then Thunder added in appreciation. "Your smoke had nice flavor." They were almost to the shore.

"It's called 'tobacco,'" he smiled, pulling a small bag out of his shirt pocket. "I would be glad to share this with you." The bow of the boat slid up on the gravel beach, but Thunder didn't get out immediately.

"The wind has helped me see that it would be good for me to introduce you to our Kwakiutl village, It lies three rivers from here." He pointed north. "I will be there in four days. You can follow the markers."

"Does your village have food they might share?" Xander asked, now with a new interest.

"They do not want shiny worthless trinkets, or medicine water; but they are a very blessed village. There is usually more than enough deer strips, seal and red fish strips. They have a large garden that produces beans and corn and squash. They might trade some of it for blankets, needle and thread. I'm sure they would trade for the shiny knives or the chopping tool, or an iron pot." The conversation was becoming seriously important to both men.

Xander asked, "Why will it take you four days to get to your village?"

"It's a long walk," Thunder answered, and I must talk with the wind.

"If you ride with us," Xander almost giggled, "We can be there this evening. The wind will take us. I must tell you that we have very little food left. That's why we ate clams. The Captain, that's our Chief, is afraid we might need to return home if we can't find supplies, food." He said for clarity.

They discussed a bit more before Thunder said he must go to the Long House for his walking stick and personal things he had stored there.

Xander, feeling some urgency to return to the boat with a now agreeable translator suggested, "If you want to leave the stick, we can find another for you."

Thunder leveled a frown at Xander, saying, "There is no other stick like this. I have had it since I was a boy. I have used it in combat, in fact, two days ago it was this stick that took the life of the Trapper before I sliced his throat. This may be my only valued possession. If anyone touches it, I will cut off their fingers. If they try to steal it, I will cut off their arm. The last person who tried to steal it is now a one-eyed Inuit." The account may have been a bit of a lie, but a useful one." He turned and headed up the hill.

When he returned, Xander learned more of this complicated and quiet man. Not only was he carrying his walking stick, but a hide robe and the Trapper's rifle. He also had a gathering bag containing enough deer strips for each member of the crew, a gift from the Skookumchuck. He now understood that a Shaman cares for anyone in trouble, perhaps everyone.

Back aboard the ship, Xander explained what he had learned from Thunder, The Trapper's rifle was secured in the armory; and the crew was warned to respect Thunder's walking stick. The deer strips were given to the grateful cook with the instructions to make them last two days. Thunder's robe was placed on the quarterdeck, and orders were given to haul the anchor and get underway, while he tried to stay out of the way as he watched the mysterious process.

Aboard the Ship

When the first sail was set, pulling the bow around toward the open water, Thunder wanted to clap his hands with joy. Then the large sails hung from the big tree opened and filled with the wind. He did clap then, much to the entertainment of those nearby. Slowly the huge ship began to make headway. Soon they were clearing the rocks and Thunder could see the big water again. The wind shifted to a more southerly direction, which was very helpful. Thunder saw it as a sign the wind was happy. By mid morning they had passed the first river mouth, and by the time the sun was overhead, Thunder pointed out the large marker that he had set so long ago. They turned toward the Morning Mountains, adjusted the sails and continued to draw closer to the Kwakiutl village. Now Thunder knew the way home, and so did the wind.

Nearly adjacent to the waterfall, the ship's anchor was lowered and orders were given to take advantage of this fresh water by cleaning the ship completely. The warm afternoon had great promise as the boat was lowered for Xander and another sailor, who carried a smoke stick, one of the lesser Chiefs, and Thunder. It was an easy trip to the sandy beach. There Thunder explained that the Kwakiutl village was a short walk up the hill.

The four had only gone part way when Thunder heard a shrill bird call, which was answered by another from the opposite side of the trail. He raised his hand to signal the others to stop. "I think we should stand very still for a moment. The Wasps have found us." He told Xander to make sure the one with the smoke stick made no aggressive motion. They waited. Very soon four young men stepped out of the brush. They all carried bows, with arrows at the ready.

"What do you want here," the leader said in an extra loud voice. They walked closer to those standing carefully still, looking quite angry. "We do not welcome Outsiders," his loud voice added.

Thunder spoke in Kwakiutl, "Do you know me?"

The loud voice said, "No, go away!"

Thunder held out his walking stick, saying, "Have you seen this before?" His tone was less patient.

Recognition was almost immediate. "Shaman Thunder!" He waved the others to put down their bows. "I'm very sorry to offend you. It has been a long while since you have been in your Long House. I will tell the others you are on your way." He whirled and the four ran full speed up the trail. The three from the ship were amazed at the encounter, and the instant response to their strange host, and his walking stick. Xander was impressed even more by this quiet Shaman.

By the time the four from the ship arrived there was quite a welcoming crowd. Slow Bear even had his singing drum to make a happy sound. Chief Sky stood in the trail with an open-arm embrace, saying, "My brother, my heart is happy to see you again." Standing just behind him was Carry, Thunder's sister. Her smile reflected the same tender welcome. Just behind her was a tall man with a wide smile and one eye.

"Is he the Inuit?' an alarmed Xander asked very quietly.

Thunder introduced Xander to Chief Sky. "He speaks Haida like a youth," the Shaman joked. "He will translate for the others who speak none of our language. I am hoping that we can find a bit of food for these guests this evening, and then meet with the council tomorrow afternoon. You look well my brother, the Chief." There was another fond embrace. "Will you join us for a steaming cup before the sun sets?"

On the way to the Long House, Thunder led the other three to the site of the village garden now in full sprout. It was a very impressive sight. By the time they arrived at the Long House, a fire had been set outside, and inside, with a large tray of deer strips and seed cakes. With the flap open to the afternoon sun, Thunder first spread his hands in greeting to his lodge, then invited his guests to be seated on the robes that were spread around the fire. Speaking to Xander, he suggested a translation for the others.

Fair Dealings

"You can see we have a very healthy village." He waited for the words to be translated. "For many years, the only trouble we have had is from Outsiders." Once again he waited for the translation, which was expanded to explain "Outsiders."

"I'm certain there is enough surplus food here to meet your present emergency." He paused again. "The question will be are you willing to deal fairly with these people?"

"They have no need to feed your ship without compensation." "If you think that way, you should go home." There was no animosity in his tone. "On the other hand, if you trade fairly with them, I believe it will be beneficial for both." After an extra long pause, he concluded, "I will continue with you for a season. I have no knowledge of the land north of here, or the villages we might find, but I will be your translator, and help you find food along the way." Xander was delighted to give the officer that message. Thunder served them the food with pouches of water, but he put steaming bags on for the anticipated visit from the Chief.

In the twilight the four Wasps escorted the visitors back to the waterfall and their boat. It was obvious to the three guests that these young warriors took their duties quite seriously, They led the way in silence and as soon as they were sure the guests were en route back to the large floating lodge, they silently turned back toward the village.

By the time the council met they had an ample opportunity to inventory their surplus food, and Xander had been carefully instructed how much the ship could offer. Both sides would have liked more, so it must have been an appropriate compromise. When Thunder said it was a time to remember, a time for prayer, each man sitting in the circle agreed. He said the smoke pipe was appropriately filled with some familiar leaves, and some tobacco from Xander. They would be blended in the smoke, as they might be in the future.

Thunder went out to find a burning coal that he could put in the smoke pipe bowl. He handed the pipe to Chief Sky with a graceful motion, saying, "A time for prayer, a happy time to remember." The Chief drew a puff and glanced at Thunder, for the flavor was much richer. He released the smoke and passed the pipe along. Each man had a different experience. For those accustomed to the pipe it was a new rich aroma; for those from the ship, it was being included with a lovely ceremony with those whom they had considered savages. When the pipe came back to Thunder, he lifted it to his eyes, glancing at each man present; before he drew in his puff of smoke, he said, "You are my brothers," and released it through his nose. His eyes were brimming tears. It was truly a time of prayer, a happy time to remember

The exchange served both sides well. There was a new wool blanket for every lodge, a new luxury. Three shiny blades that would be used in cutting strips, and a great iron pot for the Long House. There were incidentals like buttons, needles and thread to be shared, and perhaps best of all, the ship sent its empty potato sacks, many of which had leftover potatoes that had gone to sprout. Slow Bear was instructed to chop the tubers into small pieces, each with a sprout, and place them in the ground all around the garden. In the fall each plant would produce a large number of new tubers. The cycle would continue as long as they planted the left-over eyes. The empty sacks would hold the food from the gathering bags, making room for another harvest.

When the sailors from the boat came to receive their seven large bags of food, the village once again gave a friendly greeting. Slow Bear played his singing drums, and the Wasps escorted them from and to the waterfall. The Kwakiutl would be remembered as a friendly, and gracious village that was most supportive to their Outsider guests. Especially when those guests agreed to return in the Autumn on their way back home. They would need more food for their long journey.

A Summer Cruise

The days of Thunder aboard the H.M.S. Alert, are chronicled elsewhere. Let it be noted that he served the ship in many ways from helping to find edibles to caring for the sick, and injured. He aided in conversations with Haida and Inuit villages, guiding them through discussions that were frequently angry, but never hostile. In fact, his knowledge of the Outsider language was so perfected, that frequently the Chiefs spoke to him rather than the crew. Xander also perfected his knowledge of both Haida and Salish. The ship explored waterways never before seen by Outsiders, perhaps by no one at all.

Finally, when the days were growing shorter and the trees were spectacular in their bright colors, the H.M.S. Alert returned to the river beside the Morning Mountains, to acquire their food stores for their trip home. Thunder was so eager to see his family and return to the Haida village that he did not preside over the final transaction between the ship and village. He was confident they would be fair with one another. The Chief had given him two shiny discs, saying they were "gold pieces," which had little meaning to Thunder so he traded one of them to Xander for two more pouches of tobacco.

He had not asked for, nor expected compensation for the big walk in the wind. He found his canoe still hidden in slow Bear's abandoned and overgrown village. It was evening when he arrived at the Nanoose Bay. He cold camped, eager to be on his way in the morning.

Huge Trouble

The trail that he had used often seemed more worn than he recalled; there were even signs that something heavy had been dragged along it. He was prepared to skirt the Salish village when the soft breeze caught this attention. It was from the north, and growing stronger. The trees sighed with it, and a second puff was stronger. Thunder changed his direction, heading for the unfriendly village.

What he found was devastation. Reading the signs in the dirt, many men had gathered on this shoulder above the village. One or two giant smoke sticks had spit death upon the lodges. Perhaps the smaller smoke sticks had joined in the attack. Thunder hurried on to see what assistance he could be.

The first lodge he came to was hanging in tatters, empty. The next was the same. He could smell a cooking fire so he hurried on toward the Long House. When he got there, he found it also destroyed, but there were several people huddled near it. As he approached, Chief Arrow stood up slowly. It was apparent that he had been wounded.

"Chief Arrow," Thunder spoke quietly. "Your village has been ravaged. May I help you, or your survivors?"

He knelt, opening his gathering bag which had a good selection of leaves that might be useful.

"It was a nightmare," the Chief muttered, as he slumped back down on the ground. "First the terrible thunder, and death rained down everywhere." He spoke softly, unable to grasp the reality around him. "People ran, but fell, struck down. It kept pounding fire, smoke, and death." A shudder shook the young Chief. "The men charged up the hill at the enemy but the smoke sticks chopped them down like weeds. I saw my lodge, with my family in it, torn to shreds by some impossible beast." Tears ran down his cheeks unnoticed. "We have buried most. The women are still burying the children." He looked at Thunder with unfocused eyes.

The Shaman was assessing his wounds. "Chief, I must remove the nails that have pierced your flesh. I am sorry to cause you more pain. They must come out or you will die from the poison."

The Chief waved his hand absently. "I have nothing to live for; my family is gone and the village destroyed. I am ready to die." His head slumped lower.

"Perhaps that is true," the Shaman said just above a whisper, "but you are still Chief Arrow of this village. There are survivors who need your direction. They need the hope that only you can provide. I pledge to stand with you. We have lost a great deal; but there is still a need for you, Chief. May I repair your wounds. In resignation, the Chief laid back so the removal of two nails in his chest could begin. There was also a round object in his back that Thunder removed, with the aid of the shiny knife. He ground some Bleeder into a paste that was pressed into the wounds. It was the best he could do, for the moment.

He refreshed the fire, and tried to make a quick repair on the Long House, providing a shelter for the survivors. Then he scoured the village, seeking those who needed wounds tended, and sending the others to the Long House. He discovered three women who seemed to be uninjured who were willing to help find food.

Thunder struggled for four days to bring healing to the wounded. Three more were too weak to survive. They were buried beside all the others. In all, there were eight men, eleven women, three children, and Chief Arrow that survived the attack of the Spaniards, who sought punishment for a perceived insult. The Salish had refused to trade away the only food they had.

Before the winter rains set in they had banded together to make fourteen lodges from the salvage of the entire village. It was a new beginning, and they were a strong people. Thunder finally decided he could walk in the wind, and return to his own lodge, gratefully. The seasons follow one another like children dancing, and sometimes weeping.

Finis: Book Four: Defense of the Nation

Epilogue

The area of the Morning Mountains (central British Columbia coast, north of Howe Sound) became a predominant gathering place for the tribes. All who settled in the fertile valleys were prosperous, and strong enough in their unity that Outside influence was minor. Potlatch became an annual celebration, with each village represented by their tribal heritage.

The museum of Labor and Industries in Victoria B.C. has on display a walking stick dated from the fifteenth century of the modern era. It is crafted of Hazelnut wood, with a white quartzite stone imbedded in the handle, and many other attractive trimmings.

Alexander Fraser Boxer, Royal Navy, became master of the H.M.S. Alert until his retirement, when he returned to this region to operate a Trading Station. His knowledge of the people and language became legendary.

The tales of Slow Bear, the storyteller, live on in the First Nation legends. Partial collections are common in modern bookstores.

Printed in the United States
By Bookmasters